Wilderness
Peril

Wilderness Peril

THOMAS J. DYGARD

WILLIAM MORROW AND COMPANY
NEW YORK

1 2 3 4 5 6 7 8 9 10

Library of Congress Cataloging in Publication Data
Dygard, Thomas J. Wilderness peril.
Summary: Two teenage boys camping in the Minnesota woods encounter a
desperate airline hijacker attempting to escape with three-quarters of a million
dollars. [Camping—Fiction. 2. Hijacking of aircraft—Fiction. 3. Minnesota—
Fiction] I. Title.
PZ7.D9893Wh   1985   [Fic]   84-25577
ISBN 0-688-04146-9

This book is dedicated,
as is everything,
to Patty

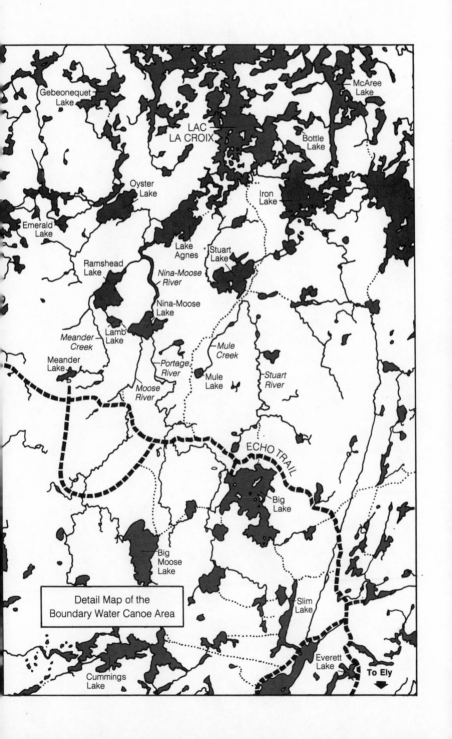

Detail Map of the
Boundary Water Canoe Area

DAY ONE

THE TRIP
Todd and Mike

Todd Barkley and Mike Roper were driving through northern Wisconsin, heading toward the Minnesota border, when they heard the news bulletin on the radio.

Todd was at the wheel of the black Blazer, with the red aluminum canoe strapped overhead, and Mike was leaning forward in the passenger seat, twirling the dial of the radio. Behind them the bed of the Blazer was laden with camping gear—a pair of rolled-up sleeping bags, an orange four-man tent rolled and tied, two Paul Bunyan packs, a green-painted plywood canoe box, a Styrofoam ice chest, and canteens. Above them the summer sky was a cloudless blue. The air rushing through the open windows of the Blazer was cooling, and it carried the clean smell of the north woods.

For Todd and Mike, this smell was a familiar one, and it was good. This was the third summer they had loaded Todd's canoe on his parents' Blazer and headed away from their homes in the Chicago suburbs for two weeks of canoeing and camping in the Boundary Waters Canoe Area of northeastern Minnesota and southern Ontario.

The cool snap of the air and the fresh smell of the woods brought back memories for Todd—the breezes whispering through the tall birch trees at night; the thrill of landing a northern pike; the beavers building their dams; the sightings of deer, moose, and bear; the clear waters of the lakes; the cry of a loon in the night; the crackle of the campfire; the cozy comfort of the sleeping bag after a day's paddling; and the quiet of it all, so very quiet.

Todd frowned as the scenes ran through his mind. There was a good chance this would be the last summer he and Mike would load up and head for two weeks in the woods. Although he did not like to think so, there was no getting around it. He and Mike had graduated from high school. Upon returning from the camping trip they were heading for college—Todd to Purdue University and Mike to Iowa State. Close friends all through high school, they had talked about attending the same college. But Mike, planning to study business administration, had the offer of a football scholarship, which sealed his decision for him. With an older brother already in college and a younger sister coming along behind him, Mike was on a tight budget for college. He needed the football scholarship. Todd, aiming for a degree in aeronautical engineering, was sure Purdue was the only place for him. The nonresident tuition was high, but he had promised his parents he would get a job to help make ends meet, and they had agreed to the out-of-state school. So Todd and Mike were heading for different worlds.

In a way, they had been in different worlds throughout

their high-school friendship—the brawny Mike, a tackle on the football team, and the angular, rangy Todd, a student who actually enjoyed math and confined his athletic endeavors to canoeing and camping. The differences between the two always had seemed, in a strange way, to firm up the friendship. Not in competition with each other, they enjoyed each other. But now the two different worlds were going to be hundreds of miles apart. Todd knew that, realistically, the friendship was bound to fade, each with his own new friends, his own new interests, in his new home at college. Sure, they had promised to stay in touch over the school year, keep up the friendship, get together over the holidays and during the summer vacations. But things were never going to be the same again. Todd was sure of it.

The chance for this final trip had meant so much to both of them that they had quit their summer jobs early —Todd's in the kitchen at Joe's Burger House and Mike's at the refreshment stand at the Merabelle movie theater. Neither of them, facing the expense of college, could really afford to lose even just two weeks' salary. But without either of them saying so, they had seemed to agree that this one last trip was worth it. Todd wondered now if he had made the right decision. After all, Mike had the help of a football scholarship, but he himself didn't.

"Hey, man, you're frowning," Mike said, leaning back in the seat. The plaintive strains of a country-western song came out of the radio. "You ought to be smiling. We're heading for the woods, and we've got Willie Nelson singing to us. What more could you want?"

Todd managed a grin. "Good ol' Willie," he said.

Todd took his foot off the accelerator and let the Blazer slow to thirty miles an hour at the edge of a small town. Inside the town, the highway bore the name "Main Street." As they drove through, Todd watched the people. The men on the sidewalk were wearing sport shirts open at the neck. Back home in the Chicago area, where he had grown up, men wore a necktie and coat in public, no matter what the temperature. Most of the vehicles on the streets of the small town were pickup trucks. Todd was surprised by the number of them with a woman at the wheel. Back home, nobody had a pickup truck. The Blazer was considered an oddity by his neighbors. Todd wondered, as he had in previous years, about life in these small towns on the edge of the north woods. All he knew for sure was that it must be very different from his own life in the Chicago suburbs. Different, and maybe better. Who could tell?

Coming out of the town, Todd speeded up to fifty-five miles an hour on the narrow, straight road. The air was smelling better every mile of the way. The trees were getting taller. The sky seemed clearer. The weather was cooler.

"We'll be there by dark, easy," Todd said.

"Yeah."

Each year Todd and Mike planned their twelve-hour drive so they would arrive at the edge of the Boundary Waters Canoe Area around sunset. The road from Ely, the little town that was the jumping-off place, to the BWCA was lined with campgrounds. The boys liked to

4

spend the first night on the edge and then get an early start the next morning, plunging into the wilderness. That way, they could put two or three lakes behind them with time left for pitching camp and perhaps an hour of fishing or exploring. With each stream they paddled and each lake they crossed, the number of campers fell off sharply. The one-day campers packed the edge or possibly ventured down a stream to a lake, complete with children and sometimes a crying baby, folding chairs and tables, and cots. But there were few people on the second lake, and even fewer on the third. Only an occasional canoeist, and maybe a far-off campfire at night, dotted the fourth lake. They would be four lakes into the woods on the second day without hurrying themselves.

The song on the radio came to an end.

An announcer's voice, twangy and not at all like the pear-shaped tones of the Chicago radio announcers, came on. "We have a news bulletin just in from the Associated Press," he said. "A hijacker has taken command of a Global Airways 727 jetliner on the ground at the Minneapolis–St. Paul airport, and is demanding a cash ransom of three-quarters of a million dollars. The hijacker reportedly is carrying a bomb. FBI agents have surrounded the plane. There is no immediate information on the number of passengers aboard the plane. Stay tuned for further details as they become available."

Kenny Rogers began singing.

Todd glanced at Mike. "Hmm," he said.

"That's a lot of money—three-quarters of a million bucks," Mike said. "Do you think they'll pay it?"

"What would you do?"

"If he's crazy, he could kill a lot of people."

"And himself."

"If he's crazy, that might not matter to him."

"There's no guarantee he won't blow 'em up even if he gets the money."

"Yeah, I guess so."

"I wonder how he thinks he's going to get away," Todd said, thinking through the hijacking logically. "You know, even if they give him the money, they're not going to just step back and let him walk away."

"He must be crazy."

"He's bound to have a plan."

"That's sure a lot of money," Mike repeated.

"Uh-huh, if he pulls it off." Todd was always the more sceptical of the two.

They drove on for ten minutes, only the country-western music breaking the hum of the engine and the singing of the tires on the blacktop. To their left, the sun was beginning to drop in the west. Ahead, some fluffy white clouds drifted lazily across the sky. They were seeing more cars now with canoes tied atop them.

"Looks like everybody in the world is heading for the BWCA," Mike said.

"It's big enough for 'em all," Todd said. "Besides, nine out of ten of them won't go past the second lake."

Mike twisted around in the seat and reached over the back. "I'm going to have a soda. Want one?"

"Not right now, thanks."

Mike extracted a can from the ice chest, popped the lid, and took a long swallow.

6

The announcer's voice came back on the radio: "Here's more on the hijacker who has taken command of the Global Airways 727 jetliner at the Minneapolis–St. Paul airport. Global Airways has announced that it will deliver the cash ransom—three-quarters of a million dollars—demanded by the hijacker. The airline also says it has agreed to certain other demands of the hijacker but declined to say what they were, explaining that the safety of the passengers and crew was involved. Stay tuned for further details as they become available."

"Uh-huh, so they're going to pay him off," Mike said. He took another swig of the soda. "That is one big bunch of money."

"He's got a plan," Todd said matter-of-factly. "Did you hear that bit about 'other demands'? That's got to do with his getaway plan."

"I guess. But he's got to be crazy." Mike paused. "Maybe thinking about that much money can make a guy crazy."

Todd grinned. "I can't even imagine that much money."

"Neither can I. Oh, wait a minute, yes, I can. It's lots and lots."

They both laughed.

Only the flickering orange flames of the campfire broke the darkness. And the only sound that broke the silence was the soft burbling of water boiling in a can on the fire.

Todd and Mike, cups in hand, sat cross-legged next to the campfire, sipping hot tea. Mike was wearing an Iowa State sweatshirt, a souvenir of a campus visit, and Todd a light blue Windbreaker. Even in August, night in the north woods was chilly. Their faces were bright, then shadowed, in the dancing glow from the fire.

The camp was pitched. The orange tent with the purple fly was visible in the campfire's light. And beyond, the black Blazer gave off an eerie reflection in the shadows. Dinner was over—steaks out of the ice chest, the last red meat Todd and Mike were going to see for two weeks. From now on, freeze-dried food was the staple of the menu. And, with luck, they would enjoy filet of northern pike rolled in cornmeal and fried in shortening. Above them the stars sparkled in the clear sky.

Todd put his cup on the ground, tilted his denim cap back on his head, and looked up at them.

"Remember last year when we picked blueberries for the pancakes?" Mike said.

"Yeah, we'll have to do that again."

"Uh-huh."

"But not tomorrow morning. I'll bet these bushes are all picked clean, what with all these people here."

"The next morning, then."

"Yeah, if the bears haven't stripped all the bushes," Todd said. "I'm about ready to hit the sack."

"Me, too."

They got to their feet. Todd took the can of water off the campfire and began breaking up the coals with the point of a folding camp shovel.

"Wait a minute," Mike said. "Before we douse things, let's see if we can find out what happened to our hijacker."

8

"Sure."

With a flashlight's beam pointing the way, they walked to the Blazer and got in. Leaving the door open so they could see by the dome light, Mike turned on the radio. The country-western station they had brought in so clearly in northern Wisconsin had long since faded. Mike twirled the dial. A station's soft rock sound came in with a strong signal.

"Okay?"

"Okay."

They sat for ten minutes, listening to the music and watching a full moon rise, casting its beam through the tall trees.

"Better start the engine," Todd said. "I don't know what this might do to the battery."

Mike, sitting behind the wheel, turned the key and brought the engine to life. Looking at his watch in the beam of the dome light, he said, "Almost on the hour— ten o'clock. Maybe they'll have a newscast then."

The song ended and an announcer's voice came on. "First, the latest about the hijacking at the Minneapolis– St. Paul airport. After almost six hours on the ground under the command of the hijacker, the Global Airways 727 jetliner, with the hijacker and the crew aboard, has taken off, destination unknown. The hijacker is in possession of the three-quarters of a million dollars cash ransom he demanded. Police officers made the delivery to the plane this evening. A short time after the money was tossed on board in two canvas bags, the hijacker freed all the passengers, holding only the crew members as hos-

9

tages. A half-hour later, he ordered the plane to take off. We'll keep you up to date on developments. Now, elsewhere in the news tonight . . ."

Mike turned off the radio. "Jeez, he got away with it."

"Well, so far."

"Yeah, so far."

"I wonder where he thinks he's going."

"Cuba," Mike said with a little laugh. "Isn't that where they all go?"

"I guess."

They walked to the tent.

"Look at that moon, will you?" Todd said.

"Yeah. We don't even need the flashlight."

THE WOODS
The Man

The man stood in the small clearing, ghostlike in the soft, pale light of the full moon.

He loosened the belts on two canvas bags strapped around his shoulders and let them fall to the ground. They landed with a heavy thudding sound. He freed himself of the parachute harness and dropped it lightly to the ground. He stood quite still for a moment, listening to the sounds of the night in the woods. Everything sounded normal—the soft whisper of the breeze in the trees, the mysterious clicking sounds in the distance that were probably small animals moving about. Then he turned slowly, all the way around, staring into the darkness surrounding him. A campfire's glimmer was sure to carry for miles in the dark woods. But there was none to be seen.

He stretched his arms above his head and grinned. "Lucky, lucky, lucky," he said in a whisper. "All these trees, and I don't land in a one of them."

He had fully expected to land in a tree, and coming down, had braced himself for it. He wasn't worried. He had landed in trees before and could do it again. This time, at least, he was being well paid for landing in a tree. But then, coming down, he had seen the clearing in the moonlight and had guided himself toward it. For a brief moment, he had felt a sharp pang of alarm. He thought he had erred. What if the clearing turned out to be a pond of water? But no, he had told himself, the moonlight would be glistening off the still surface of a pond, and there was no gleaming reflection. Drifting lower, he saw the shadows of bushes, and his last doubts vanished. But then for another brief moment there had been a second pang of alarm. Campers liked clearings. Clearings offered a bit of breeze, chasing the bugs away. What if he landed in somebody's campsite? But the thoughts that raced through his mind then delivered a reassuring message: canoe campers never went this far away from a lake for their campsite. He was okay, so far.

"Lucky, lucky, lucky," he repeated.

In the distance, a loon called. Then the soft breeze rippling through the trees shifted direction, carrying away its cries.

The man peeled off his blue suit-jacket and dropped it on the ground. He unbuckled his belt and unbuttoned his blue suit-trousers, and stepped out of them. Next to come off were his necktie and shirt. Standing in the moonlight in jeans and a khaki camping shirt, he stretched his arms over his head. He felt better with the removal of the bulky outer layer of clothing.

He was not tall—maybe five feet ten inches—but he had a sturdy build. His frame had the packed-in look of muscle. He had the easy, fluid movements of an athlete. He wore a beard; both the beard and the hair on his head were jet black.

The man reached into his jeans pocket and pulled out a penlight. Without turning it on, he dug into the other pocket and took out a compass. He squatted on his haunches, holding the compass flat in the palm of his left hand, and turned on the penlight. After squinting down at the compass and then switching off the light, he turned his head in the direction of the needle. North was uphill, through a clump of birch trees outlined in the light of the full moon.

The man stood up, took a deep breath, and started walking north. He counted the paces—"one, two, three . . . forty-one, forty-two . . . sixty-three, sixty-four . . ."

He stopped, turned left at a right angle, and resumed pacing.

Six times he paced, stopped, turned left, and finally found himself back where he had started—at the pile of clothes, the two canvas bags, and the harness of the parachute with lines trailing off into the darkness.

He nodded slightly, as if agreeing with himself, and said, "Okay, I'm all to myself. All alone. I don't know where, but I'm all to myself." He was smiling. "And I'm rich."

The man bent, picked up the harness of the parachute, and began pulling in and rolling up the rippling wave of white silk. Once in hand, he carried the parachute to the edge of the clearing and shoved it under a clump of bushes. Then he collected his pile of clothing and stuffed it in behind the parachute under the bushes as well.

Returning to the clearing, he picked up the canvas bags by the straps, one in each hand. He hefted the bags slightly, as a man might test a bowling ball he was thinking of buying. Then he walked across the clearing and stashed the bags with the other things.

Back in the center of the clearing, he sat down on the ground. From a shirt pocket he extracted a throwaway razor and a small tube of shaving cream. He frowned at the razor. This was going to be worse than the jump—shaving dry. But the beard had to go, no question. And it had to go right away. The shaving cream would help, maybe.

He unbuttoned his khaki camping shirt and slipped out of it, placing it on the ground beside him. Naked above the waist, he shivered slightly in the cool breeze.

He opened the tube of shaving cream and squeezed a stick of it onto his left hand. He began rubbing the shaving cream into the beard—under his sideburns, across his cheek, down over his jaw, onto the upper throat, his chin, then the other side of his face. Once he stopped, laying down the razor, and fished the penlight out of his pocket. He flicked it on and turned the beam on his left hand. Yes, the dye that had turned his blond beard black was coming off in the shaving cream. Messy. But nothing else to do. He pulled a handkerchief out of his hip pocket and wiped the shaving cream, now gray with black streaks of dye, off his hand. Then he began shaving the beard off, slowly, slowly. No nicks, please.

Finally finished, the man wiped his face with the handkerchief, then flashed the penlight on the handkerchief—one tiny spot of blood. Not bad. He had felt the nick when it happened. Upper lip. No problem. He rubbed his face with his hands. He was glad the beard was gone. He never had liked it.

He got to his feet and looked around, as if somewhere in the darkness there was an indication of what to do next. The trees and bushes around the clearing cast spooky shadows in the powdery moonlight.

The man glanced at the bushes that hid the suit, parachute, and the money bags. First thing in the morning he had to hide them better—cover them with leaves, loose dirt, maybe a little digging with his camping knife. Not much covering was needed. Just enough to keep them from being spotted from the air. No problem.

Then he needed to find a body of water. He had shaved without water because the beard had to go—and without delay. But he could not rinse the dye out of his hair without water.

He needed water, too, in order to meet up with a canoeist who could tell him his location. He needed to know where he was. And there were no road signs in the woods.

He glanced north, up the hill. He shook his head slightly. "No, not there, not that way," he whispered to himself. He knew that in this wilderness, no matter where a person was, water was not far away—a stream meandering lazily between a pair of lakes, or one of the hundreds of lakes themselves. He knew, too, that the closest water was not to be found by going uphill. He looked downhill, pulled out the compass, and flashed the penlight's beam on it briefly. He lifted his gaze from the compass, following a line opposite the needle's point.

"That's the way—south," he said aloud.

The man walked out of the clearing and into the woods, seeking a place to sleep that offered a protective cover against the eyes that were sure to be peering down into the woods from airplanes at first daylight.

THE AIRPORT
Agent Stoneham

The room was a madhouse. Officially designated "VIP Lounge," it was beautifully decorated—luxurious sofas and chairs, heavy cocktail tables, thick carpeting, large lamps that cast soft glows of light. The purpose of the room was to offer comfort and privacy—especially privacy—for celebrities passing through the Minneapolis–St. Paul airport. It served as a haven beyond the reach of the clamoring public for movie stars, politicians, famous athletes. But for the ninety-six passengers freed from Global Airways Flight 681 before the hijacker and the crew took off, the VIP Lounge was anything but a haven. It was bedlam.

Ted Stoneham, special agent in charge of the Minneapolis FBI office, stood at one side of the room watching the milling throng of people—the angry, the frightened, the frustrated.

On the other side of the room a young man with straight brown hair, his necktie loosened, was standing on one of the heavy cocktail tables trying to get the attention of the crowd.

"If you'll just be quiet a moment," he shouted. "Please,

please, let me have your attention. If you'll just be quiet a moment, we'll be able to begin processing everyone out of here and getting you on your way."

A woman standing near him looked up and asked in a voice that was almost a shriek, "Who are you?"

"I'm with Global Airways," the man said, his voice rising in the hope that all could hear him. "Please, please, be quiet, and we can get under way." He paused and appeared relieved that the chattering and murmuring seemed to be dying away. But the pause was a mistake. Suddenly a dozen voices from all sides erupted in the moment of silence. The man lifted his hands to signal for quiet again, but it was too late.

"My luggage is aboard that plane that took off," a man shouted.

"Get under way with what?" another man called out in a tone of disgust. "I've already missed my connection in Chicago. What more do you want?"

In the back of the crowd a baby began crying.

"Can't I just use a telephone?" a woman asked.

The man from the airline kept his hands up, waving them, trying to quiet the crowd. Finally the voices died down again. The man did not make the mistake again of pausing; he spoke quickly. "These men are with the FBI," he said, gesturing in Stoneham's direction. The heads in the crowd turned and looked. "They will want your names, addresses, telephone numbers, and any information you might be able to offer that might lead to the identification of the hijacker. It won't take long, and—"

"It'll take all night," said the man who had complained

that his luggage was aboard the hijacked plane.

The young man glared down at him. Then he continued as if he had not been interrupted. "The agents will be interviewing you at that table over there," he said, pointing toward a long narrow table with a lamp standing at one end. Some of the people in the crowd began moving toward the table, trying to wedge themselves into a place at the head of the line. "And," the man continued, "after you've been interviewed by the agents, please stop at this table over here"—he gestured toward another table —"where Global Airways personnel will be ready to help you with your revised travel plans."

A woman wearing a Global Airways uniform entered the room and walked past Stoneham to the brown-haired man. Without stepping down from the cocktail table, he leaned over, hands on knees, to hear her message. She spoke softly into his ear. He nodded slightly, then stood up and held out his hands. "Ladies and gentlemen, just a moment. Quiet, quiet. Just one more thing." He waited for the shuffling and the chatter to stop. "The hijacker has bailed out of the plane—parachuted out—and the plane is returning here, so you will have your luggage in hand shortly."

A murmur of comment rippled through the crowd, and then the passengers resumed their shuffling movement toward the table where Ted Stoneham's agents waited to interview them.

The young man stepped down from the cocktail table. He watched for a moment as the FBI agents began interviewing the first of the passengers in line.

Stoneham walked across and stood next to him. "Ninety-six passengers, right?"

"Yes."

Stoneham shrugged his shoulders. "That means ninety-six different descriptions."

The man smiled weakly and nodded.

"The one I want to see is the stewardess who dealt with the hijacker—the one who relayed his demands. Let me know the instant the plane lands, and get her in here."

"Sure."

"She's here."

"Where?"

"Over there. The brunette in uniform."

Ted Stoneham glanced in the direction of the young man's nod. The woman he saw was short, slender, pretty. She seemed at ease and unruffled. She did not appear at all to have been flying with a hijacker who claimed to be carrying a bomb.

"Okay, thanks." Stoneham walked across the room toward her. "Gloria Marsh?" he asked. She looked up. He showed her a badge in a leather folder. "May we talk?"

"Of course." She smiled at him.

Stoneham led her to a corner, away from the crowds jammed around the table where FBI agents were questioning passengers, and around the table where Global Airways people, with portable video terminals, were checking alternate flight arrangements. They sat in over-stuffed chairs facing each other over a cocktail table.

"Well," Stoneham said. "Everything, if you will, in your own words."

Gloria Marsh smiled at him again. For a moment she gazed past him, as if clicking the thoughts into place in her mind before speaking. Then she looked back at Stoneham and said, "He was not what you would call your ordinary, run-of-the-mill passenger."

"Oh? How so?"

"Phoney."

"Funny?"

"No, no, phoney—you know, false."

"In what way?"

"For one thing, his beard and his hair—jet black—and I'd bet anything it was a dye job. I've seen it on men before. Comb out the gray, you know."

Stoneham nodded. "Yes, what else?"

"He seemed sort of chunky, but . . ."

"But what?"

"I don't think he was chunky at all. Maybe muscular, but not chunky, and yet he looked chunky."

"What do you mean?"

"This may sound crazy, but I think he had on several layers of clothing—at least two layers."

"What you saw was a suit and tie, right?"

"Blue suit, single-breasted, no vest, white shirt, striped tie, maroon and blue."

"You're very observant."

She smiled. "You know, I've thought about the chance of something like this happening to me someday, and I always told myself that I'd memorize all the details I could."

"What else did you memorize?"

"The shoes."

"What about them?"

"Well, all I saw, of course, really, were the toes—you know, sticking out from under the cuffs of his trousers."

"And—?"

"They were tan, light tan."

"So?"

"Businessmen don't wear light tan shoes with blue business suits."

"They might."

"I guess so." She paused. "But these had those kind of humped-up toes—like, you know, work shoes."

"Or jump boots?"

"Yes, maybe like jump boots."

Stoneham nodded. "Do you think you could identify a photograph of him? I mean, if the hair color was different, and maybe there was no beard, and we showed you a picture of the real Mister X, could you identify him?"

The stewardess shrugged her shoulders slightly. "I think so," she said finally. "The eyes . . ."

"What about the eyes?"

"I don't know. It's just that eyes are sort of like fingerprints—no two pairs of eyes are alike, you know?" Then she added, almost parenthetically, "He had nice eyes." She laughed softly.

Stoneham did not laugh. "He could have disguised the eye color easily enough with contact lenses."

"Color is not what I meant. I'd remember those eyes."

"Good. Okay. We'll try to come up with some pictures for you to look at."

"Do you have any idea who he is?"

Stoneham looked at her sharply. He was the questioner and she the answerer, and not the other way around. But instead of ignoring her question, as he frequently did in interviewing witnesses, he said, "Not yet."

"I know one other thing about him," she said.

"What's that?"

"He's from east Texas."

"What?"

"He's from east Texas. That's where I'm from—Marshall, Texas—and his accent was the same as mine; I grew up hearing it. He's from somewhere around east Texas. I'd bet on it."

Stoneham smiled at her. "You've been a big help," he said. "We'll be back in touch with you."

Gloria Marsh nodded slightly and returned his smile. "Any time," she said.

The last of the passengers were passing from the FBI to the Global Airways table. The young man with the brown hair was with them, murmuring something designed to calm their anger at being near the end of the line.

Ted Stoneham dropped into a chair at the table with the FBI agents and watched the dwindling line at the Global Airways table. "Anything?" he asked.

One of the agents managed a half grin. "Ninety-six passengers and ninety-six descriptions," he said. "Our man was either fat or thin, tall or short, no doubt about it. Somebody thought he had a foreign accent. About the only thing everyone agreed on was that he had a beard."

Stoneham snorted softly. "The only thing about him that doesn't matter—the beard," he said. "For sure, he had a beard. And now, for sure, he doesn't have a beard."

"Anything out of the stewardess?"

"Yes. Struck gold with her. She had watched and listened—kept her eyes and ears open through the whole thing—and she filled in a lot of gaps." Stoneham paused. "She thinks she might be able to recognize his eyes. And she says the man had an east Texas accent. She grew up in east Texas."

"Well, that's something."

"Uh-huh," Stoneham said. "So, we're looking for a man with jumping experience—parachute experience—and a lot of it. No beginner would have thought to demand four 'chutes, and then open and inspect three of them before strapping on the fourth one, confident that we hadn't tried to palm off a faulty 'chute on him. No, the man really knows parachutes.

"And we're looking for a man with a knowledge of 727 jets—an intimate knowledge, because he had to know how to jump the circuitry and get the back door open in flight. Not many people know how to do that.

"And," Stoneham continued with a sigh, "a man, beardless, most likely with either blond or reddish hair, muscular but probably average build, with an east Texas accent—and nice eyes, the stewardess said."

Stoneham looked at the other agents. "He shouldn't be hard to pin down, should he?"

DAY TWO

THE WOODS
Todd and Mike

The rising sun was half of an orange ball peeping over the eastern horizon.

Todd, squatting in front of the canoe stove, lifted the tin of water off the blue flame. He poured some water into a cup and dunked—and redunked—a tea bag. When the tea was strong enough, he laid the tea bag on a flat rock and sat back, savoring the hot drink. From the tent behind him, he heard Mike's even breathing.

Leaning back on an elbow, Todd sipped his tea and listened to the sounds of the morning. The air was cool, but the bright orange sun rising in a cloudless sky gave promise of a hot day with a bright glare off the lakes of the BWCA. A chipmunk, looking for breakfast, skittered in front of him.

Around him, the other campsites were coming to life. Todd heard the voice of a man, muffled by the dense foliage separating the camps. He heard the shrill voice of a woman—"Davey, Davey, come here"—and a child's laughter. Through the bushes and trees he caught glimpses of color—first red, then yellow—as people moved around near their tents.

The campsites on the edge of the BWCA always were full. There were people, such as Todd and Mike, preparing to head into the wilderness on an extended canoe trip. But there were others—sometimes single families, sometimes whole groups of them—who liked the edge of the BWCA and needed to go no farther. They camped here, enjoying the woods and the fishing on nearby lakes, while staying within easy reach of the comforts of civilization.

Todd had noticed that one type of camper group was always absent from the campsites around the edge of the wilderness: the people who were coming out of the BWCA after an extended wilderness journey. These campers did not linger for another night or two under the stars in the woods. They wanted a warm shower, a change of clothes, their own bed at home. If they were beginners, they invariably had been in the woods too long. Beginners, with their dreams of pastoral beauty and close communion with nature, always tended to overplan —too many miles and too many days—for themselves. They paid no attention to the stories of the black flies, the mosquitoes, and the rigors of paddling and portaging. Beginners coming out at the end of their canoe trips were easy to spot. They were always snappish—at their companions and at the whole world. But even veterans of the woods, like Todd and Mike, who knew how to pace themselves, were ready to head for home when they came out.

"Mornin'," Mike said, rubbing his eyes as he walked up behind Todd. "Did I oversleep?"

Todd turned and looked up at him. "Nope. It's still early. Plenty of time. Have a cup of tea. I'll get the pancakes started."

Mike poured hot water into a cup and, picking up Todd's tea bag from the flat rock, began dunking. "Looks like a hot one coming up."

"I think so."

Todd walked over to the canoe box to get the utensils for breakfast. He always did the cooking and Mike always did the cleaning up. It was a routine they fell into when they first began camping together. Todd liked to cook and, luckily, Mike did not mind the clean-up chores.

Todd extracted an iron skillet. The heavy fry-pan was a luxury on a canoe trip in the BWCA—one that Todd and Mike paid for with every portage between lakes or around rocky stretches of river. Another camper might have settled for a thin, lightweight skillet, thankful for the saving of another pound or two every time a portage loomed ahead. But Todd and Mike figured the skillet was worth its weight when, deep in the woods, they sat in the fading light of day and cooked the day's catch of northern pike. The heavy iron skillet did the job better than any other.

Todd lifted a brown paper bag out of the canoe box. It was labeled "B–1," meaning breakfast the first day. They always outlined their menus to the last detail in advance. They listed the items for each meal and packaged each meal separately. By planning carefully, they eliminated the risk of running out of any needed items. And by packaging the food for each meal separately, they

29

had a balanced diet every day from beginning to end. Who wanted to end a camping trip with nothing but apples to eat for the last two days? Too, this system enabled them to shed their paper containers as they went. The paper bags and boxes went into the campfire, no longer taking up space. They had no boxes with three potatoes rattling around in the bottom, no collection of containers with one serving apiece left in them, and no large bags holding six different items.

Todd opened the brown paper bag and took out two packets of pancake mix. He dumped the contents into a pan, poured in water from a canteen, and stirred. Then he placed the skillet on the fire and spooned out shortening from a plastic bag, dropping it on the skillet.

"Got the maps?" Todd asked.

Mike reached into the canoe box and pulled out a cardboard tube. He poked a finger into the end of the tube and slid out the rolled-up collection of maps. He unrolled them. One was large, displaying the entire BWCA—the Superior National Forest of Minnesota and the Quetico Provincial Park of Ontario. The smaller maps detailed sections of the BWCA. Mike riffled through them.

"Here's what we want."

Todd scooted the shortening around the warming skillet with a spatula and leaned over toward Mike to peer down at the map.

Mike's finger moved along a line—Moose River—to a lake: Nina-Moose Lake. Then along a line—Nina-Moose River—to a lake: Lake Agnes.

"We'll make Lake Agnes for lunch," Todd said.

"Easy, sure."

"Maybe stay there tonight, if it's not crowded. What do you think?"

"Uh-huh." Mike's finger traced a portage and a river path from Lake Agnes into Lac La Croix, a large crescent of water extending generally east-west for something like forty miles. "And there, maybe tomorrow night, huh?"

"Yeah."

Mike's finger was just below some tiny lettering: "Painted Rock." The ancient Indian markings were a landmark for the travelers on Lac La Croix.

Todd turned back to the skillet. He gave the melted shortening a gentle shove with the spatula and picked up the bowl of pancake batter. He spooned dollops of the batter onto the skillet and watched them widen into small circles. "I wonder what's happened to our hijacker," he said.

"He's probably in Cuba by now."

"Think so?"

"That's where they all go, isn't it?"

Neither of them made any move to turn on the Blazer's radio to find out. In their minds, at least, the Blazer and its radio had already been left behind. Already they were hearing the sounds of the woods, sniffing the aromas of the wilderness, feeling the breezes in their faces and the hard-packed ground of the trails under their feet. The hijacker did not matter.

THE WOODS
The Man

The man sat on the large flat rock projecting out into the lake. He hugged his knees and stared at the mirror surface of the water in the bright morning sunlight. The world around him was silent, absolutely silent. The world he watched was still, absolutely still. Then a fish broke the surface. There was the tiny sound of the splash. Ripples moved out in a perfect circle. Then the sound died out and the ripples played out. All was silent again, all was still.

The man's hair—blond, with the slightest hint of reddish-orange—was damp. He ran his hands through his hair and looked at them. No trace of the black dye. But he could not be sure. He wished he had thought to stick a small hand mirror in his pocket. Too late now. He wiped his jaw and chin with his hand and looked at it. No trace of the black dye there, either. Okay. Maybe okay.

The man scanned the distant edge of the lake. The sun was coming up behind him. He was sitting on the eastern edge of the lake, facing west. To his right—to the north of him—he saw a tiny stream emptying into the lake. Too small, probably, for canoeists. He turned his gaze back to the opposite bank. There seemed to be an opening—either the wide mouth of a stream or a connecting strait leading to another lake. He decided that probably the canoeists he needed—and was waiting for—were going to appear in that opening.

Nothing to do but wait.

He straightened his right leg and reached into his jeans pocket, extracting a small cellophane package. Tearing off the end, he took out a stick of dried beef. He looked at it. Funny, he wasn't hungry. He slowly ate the stick of dried beef anyway.

The man unbuttoned the breast pocket of his shirt and pulled out a memo book and a folded map. The memo book fell open to the back page, and the man unconsciously smiled at the confusing maze of penciled lines and circles. It was a crude schematic of the critical wiring juncture that controlled the lock on the back door of a 727 jetliner. Working properly, the wiring system made it impossible to open the door in flight. But with minimal tampering the system released its hold. Not many people could draw that schematic. But one who could, a technician he had worked with at American Airlines' maintenance center in Tulsa, Oklahoma, had been lured into it in the course of proving his point that nothing was foolproof. That had been more than a year ago. "Well," the man said to himself, smiling again, "that tech knew what he was talking about."

He leafed through the memo book until he came upon a page of scribbling—the paces and directions he had taken from his landing spot to this rock sticking out into the lake. Glancing at the numbers and the letters—*N* for north, *W* for west—he nodded slightly in approval. He knew his way back to the money.

Then he opened the map and spread it on the ground. He looked down at a thousand lakes, maybe several thousand. Who knew? And he was sitting on the eastern edge of one of them. All he needed now was one word—the name of the lake. Then, once found on the map, the lake would show him where he was located and how far he had to walk to reach the hidden stash he needed to escape the woods.

He glanced up at the opening in the far bank. No sign of life. He might have to wait all day for a canoe to pass. A remote lake, off the more popular routes, perhaps reached only by long and grueling portages, might go a long time without a canoe passing by.

The man frowned, then shrugged. "It's one of the chances you take," he said aloud.

The prospect of a long wait bothered the man for more than one reason. He knew that the longer he waited for a canoe to appear on the lake, the greater the chance the canoeists would be aware of the hijacking and the hijacker's parachute escape into the woods with the money. So he hoped for an early canoe, not only for his own comfort but for his chances of getting away.

A dull, droning sound broke the silence of the woods. The man knew the sound—the engine of a small airplane. He picked up the map and got to his feet. He backed off the rock toward the woods, all the while turning his head

34

and squinting his eyes at the horizon. He found the plane —a speck coming in at him from the north. He was off the rock and in the woods.

The man knelt by a tree and watched. The plane, white with green trim, came in low over the lake. It was equipped with pontoon landing gear, capable of touching down on water—for pursuit, for questioning, for capture of anyone suspicious.

Edging around behind the tree, out of sight, he held his breath. Had they seen him? Powerful binoculars might have picked him out at the very moment the plane became a speck to him low in the sky. This was the one stage in the getaway when he could not afford to be seen. Later, with the gear from his hidden stash, who cared? He would be just another camper. But now he was a man alone in the woods without either tent or canoe. He was also without answers, if there were questions. No, he was a goner if they spotted him, caught him, and questioned him now.

The plane roared overhead and disappeared to the south.

The man brought his head around the tree and watched the plane disappear over a stand of birch trees atop a rise in the ground. He sighed and stepped back out into the open. They had not seen him. If they had, the plane would have circled for another look, and then maybe have landed on the water for questioning. Perhaps later a picture they took during their flyover would reveal a flash of blue—his jeans—or a patch of skin or the light reddish-orange of his hair—and they would know they had flown over somebody. But that would be later, too late to matter. By that time, surely, a canoe would have appeared on the lake and he would have hailed the canoeists and found out his location. By then he would have long since been on his way.

The dull, droning sound of the airplane engine faded away.

The man walked back onto the rock projecting out into the lake. He folded the map and replaced it in his pocket, then sat down and, hugging his knees, watched the opening in the opposite bank. All was quiet and still.

HEADQUARTERS
Agent Stoneham

"Okay, okay," Ted Stoneham said. "Let's get seated and get down to business. Let's find out where we are."

He had just finished shaking hands with the collection of men in the back room of Barney's Restaurant in Ely, the tiny Minnesota town on the southern edge of the Boundary Waters Canoe Area. The back room of Barney's usually served as a private dining room for civic clubs, an occasional wedding reception, and other groups. But now it was the command center for the FBI agents, sheriff's deputies, state troopers, and rangers trying to track down and capture a hijacker and recover three-quarters of a million dollars.

At this same moment other law enforcement officers were fanning out along the roads skirting the BWCA, trying to tie a noose around the area and trap the hijacker inside.

While the men settled into their chairs on either side of a long table, Ted Stoneham took off his coat, draped it over a chair, and turned to stare at the maps thumb-tacked to the wall. A huge map displayed the entire

BWCA, and an array of smaller—but larger-scale—maps detailed takeout points and the area where they guessed the hijacker might have landed. Somebody had marked each of the major takeout points in red—an X inside a circle—and Stoneham squinted at them. There seemed to be a hundred X's. The same red pencil had marked with a series of concentric circles the approximate area of the parachutist's landing, based on the best guess of the jetliner's pilot.

Stoneham turned and sat down in the chair at the head of the table. He glanced down the table at the two rows of faces turned toward him. They were waiting. Stoneham turned to the ranking state trooper. "Is everything out there sealed off?"

"We're getting it sealed off."

Stoneham frowned. He thought of all those red circles with an X inside them. He remembered that Ely was a small town in a remote area. There were precious few state troopers stationed here, and only a few deputies operated out of the sheriff's office. Additional state troopers had moved in during the night, along with some deputies from neighboring counties; but their numbers were small compared with the job to be done. And the rangers, for the most part, were at their posts in the woods, possibly not even aware yet of a hijacker's plunge into the woods.

"How much longer?"

"Couple hours, I'm afraid."

"Okay. I hope our man is still in there."

"He will be. He couldn't do much moving around in the night."

"Yes. But he'll be moving around now, and we need to get everything in place." He paused. "Airplanes—and helicopters—are they out and working?"

There was a murmur of yeses, confirming the presence of the forest rangers' planes and the state police helicopters.

Stoneham nodded.

"Who among you knows the woods best?" he asked.

"Nobody knows it all," somebody said from the end of the table.

"But who knows it *best*?"

The men looked at each other, and finally all eyes settled on one man—a man in his fifties with short-cropped, sandy-colored hair turning to gray, a weathered face, and the squinty look around the eyes that came from years in the sun and wind. He was wearing a ranger's uniform.

"You?" Stoneham asked.

"I guess so," the man answered. "I grew up in 'em."

"Sorry, I don't remember your name."

"Lars Nillsen," he said. Then he added, "I'm a ranger."

"Yes. All right, will you tell me how you would get out of the woods if you had parachuted in last night with your arms hugging a hundred pounds of money in two canvas bags?"

Nillsen ran a hand through his hair. "Well, I . . ." He let the words trail off while he thought. The room was silent. Clearly, everyone agreed that Lars Nillsen knew more about moving around in the woods than anyone else. Stoneham waited with the rest of them.

"The way I see it," Nillsen said slowly, "it's too much for him to just carry out on foot."

Stoneham frowned. "Too much? I don't see why, if he's strong and in shape, and I think we'd better assume that he is."

"That's not what I meant," Nillsen said. "He'd stick out like a sore thumb trudging through the woods with a heavy canvas bag in each hand." He paused. "No canoe, no tent, no pack, no fishing gear—just a couple of heavy canvas bags, and afoot alone in the woods. No, sir, it's too much for him to carry and say he was just out for a walk, a little bit of exploring." He paused again. "And it's too little for him to carry and say he was on a camping trip."

"Uh-huh," Stoneham said, watching Nillsen. He made a mental note to allow Nillsen to finish in the future without interruption. The ranger spoke slowly, even hesitantly, but he made sense. "And so—?"

"Well, I'd want a canoe and all the camping gear that goes with it, if I was trying to come out of the woods with all that money, and do it without attracting attention."

Stoneham nodded. He stared at a spot high on the far wall, beyond the heads of the men in front of him. He started to say, "Ah, but our hijacker did not, to the best of our knowledge, have a canoe and all the other gear with him when he jumped out of the airplane." But he kept his mouth shut, waiting.

Nillsen seemed to anticipate Stoneham's unasked question. "If it was me," he continued, "I would have stashed it in advance." He paused and, speaking softly, added, "Or would've had my partner bring it in."

Yes, Stoneham thought, there might be an accomplice. But there would be time later to pursue that possibility.

40

Right now he wanted the rest of Nillsen's scenario. "Either way," Stoneham said, "it seems chancy—a stash somewhere in the woods."

Somebody across from Nillsen spoke up. "A man who jumps out of a hijacked airliner into the woods in the middle of the night seems to me to be someone willing to take a few chances."

Stoneham looked back at Nillsen. "I mean, how would you know where to stash your canoe . . . the gear? You would have no way of knowing exactly where you might come down. How would you be able to find your stash after landing?"

"No problem," Nillsen said.

"Why?"

"Well, if he's got a map and he's got the stash marked on it, all he has to do is find out where he's landed and he'll know which way to go to find his gear." He paused. "He can ask someone where he is, find the spot on his map, and use a compass to go in the right direction. No problem at all."

"He'd have to ask someone where he was," Stoneham said softly, almost under his breath. His detective's mind liked the idea of the fugitive having to reveal himself, even to the slight extent of asking someone, "Where am I?" Then, encouraging Nillsen to continue, Stoneham asked, "He might have a long walk, mightn't he?"

The young deputy at Stoneham's left grinned. "He might figure it was worth it," he said.

Stoneham looked back at Nillsen. "But carrying the canvas bags—he'd stick out like a sore thumb, you said."

Nillsen shrugged. "If it was me," he said, "I'd leave the money bags, go to the stash, and return for the money when I had my canoe and other gear."

"Uh-huh," Stoneham said, and frowned. The prospect of the hijacker leaving the money and returning for it later raised an unpleasant specter in his mind. The man might not return for the money for a week, a month, even a year. He might simply come out of the woods today or tomorrow, blithely passing police checkpoints with nothing more incriminating than the smile on his face. In fact, he might be walking out empty-handed at this very minute, leaving all those officers out there encircling—nothing. He then could return for the money later.

The thought seemed to occur to the others, but nobody said anything for a moment.

"Okay," Stoneham said finally, "let's assume that he's got gear stashed and he's going for it. Like you said"— he nodded at Nillsen—"he'll stick out like a sore thumb trying to walk out with nothing but a couple of heavy canvas bags."

"Do you think we're looking for one or two men coming out?" one of the deputies asked.

"One or two *persons*, not men," Stoneham corrected. "If there was a partner waiting on the ground, it might be a woman."

"A woman going in alone," Nillsen said, "well, it's pretty unlikely."

"Don't women canoe?" Stoneham asked.

Nillsen smiled at him. "Not many women want to carry a canoe all by themselves on a portage trail." He paused. "I'm not saying it's impossible, just that I don't remember ever seeing it."

"Matter of fact," said another one of the rangers, "anyone—man or woman—canoeing all alone deep inside is pretty unusual. We ought to check all the singles very closely."

Stoneham nodded. "What about cars?" He glanced at the state trooper. "People coming out of the woods are returning to their cars, aren't they? Our man is going to need transportation if he makes it to the road."

"Maybe," the state trooper said.

Nillsen spoke up. "If you mean, did he have to stash a car at a takeout point in advance to give him a means of getting away, the answer is no. Lots of people arrange pickups with the local canoe liveries."

"Wouldn't hurt to get license numbers, though."

"Okay," the state trooper said.

"And let's contact the canoe liveries."

"Sure."

"Anything else?"

Nobody spoke.

"Okay," Stoneham said. "Have your people out there question the campers coming out about anyone asking where he is, or seeing anything strange—a half-buried parachute, a stash of gear, or"—he smiled slightly—"canvas bags filled with cash."

THE WOODS
Todd and Mike

The long portage from the road to the put-in point on the Moose River—a hundred and seventy-seven rods, a little more than half a mile—was behind them. Todd and Mike, each with a Paul Bunyan pack on his back, carrying the canoe upside down above their heads, had left behind the overstocked and noisy campsites on the edge. For a moment, as they put the canoe in the water and tied down their gear, they were alone with the morning sounds of the woods. Behind them, upstream, the water rippled over an outcropping of rocks into the gentle stream below. From downstream a canoe approached with two young men in their twenties, both shirtless. They were coming out, their trip ending.

"Hey!" Todd greeted them.

"Hi!" the paddler in the bow responded.

Then Todd and Mike stepped into their canoe and pushed off, digging their paddles into the water.

In short order, two more portages loomed up before them—the first a walk of twenty rods around a jumble of rocks blocking the stream, and the second a short stretch to bypass a collection of boulders in the water.

At each, Todd and Mike leaped out of the canoe, unloaded the packs, tied the paddles in the canoe to make a carrying rack, pulled on their packs, hoisted the canoe above their heads, and walked the portage at a brisk pace.

Back in the river after the second of the portages, they paddled for Nina-Moose Lake.

Just short of the lake, they encountered an unmapped obstacle—a beaver dam. The water was backed up behind the dam, forming a wide and languid pool. At the lower points in the dam, water trickled over.

"They finished the job," Todd said with a grin.

Both of them remembered the dam, extending three-quarters of the way across the stream, from their trip a year ago. That time, passing the dam was a simple matter of steering to the left and riding the narrow and swift current through the opening, knowing that somewhere one or two hidden beavers were watching in alarm.

This time there was no opening in the dam.

Mike, in the bow, thrust his paddle straight down and brought up a gooey blob of mud. "Soft," he said.

"Let's try it on the right."

"Yeah."

Rather than leap out of the canoe into the water—and sink up to their calves in mud—they paddled toward the right bank.

At the edge they stepped out and walked the canoe to the dam. Mike, in the front, stepped over the dam and pulled on the lead rope. Todd, in the rear, followed on the bank until he was able to step on the dam. By that time

45

the canoe was over the dam, idling in the stream below. Todd held its stern while Mike stepped back into the bow. Then Todd stepped in with one foot and shoved off from the bank with the other. The canoe zipped forward in the clear water as they dipped their paddles again.

They saw their first deer of the trip on the last bend of the Moose River before the water emptied into Nina-Moose Lake. The deer, standing on the bank taking a drink, looked up with an air of unconcern as they approached, then suddenly turned and leaped away into the woods.

Paddling into the lake, Todd and Mike both instinctively glanced back at the mouth of Moose River emptying into Nina-Moose Lake. At the moment, the mouth of the river was their exit into the lake. But on the return trip, it was their entryway. They needed to be able to recognize the river from the lake side, not the river side, when they were coming out. The first rule of wilderness travel was to glance back at landmarks so they might be recognized on the return trip. So, almost without thinking, they looked back and memorized the picture from the lake side.

A stiff breeze blew across the lake. Waves, with tiny whitecaps riding atop them, rippled against the canoe's side. The waves posed no danger. They were not large enough to splash water into the canoe. But they were strong enough to shove it off course if the paddlers did not tend to business every stroke of the way.

"Let's pull over a minute," Todd said.

Mike shifted sides in his paddling, helping turn the

canoe toward a large flat rock at the lake's edge.

At the rock, each of them tied their lead rope to a branch of a sturdy bush and climbed out of the canoe. Todd leaned back in, opened his pack, and extracted a plastic ziplock bag. From it he took out a folded map and a compass. He opened the map and laid the compass on it.

Mike leaned over and watched.

The sighting was easy. Nina-Moose River, leading to Lake Agnes, flowed out of Nina-Moose Lake at a point almost due north of the rock where Todd and Mike were sitting. But the due-north reading was not what made the charting easy. The river flowed out just beyond a large peninsula protruding into the lake.

Todd, squinting across the lake, saw the projection of land clearly. "We need to point for the tip of the peninsula," he said, "and then go to the left of it."

"We're going to have to go against the wind to keep ourselves on a due-north course."

"Yeah."

They both knew that if they let the wind blow them off course and then repeatedly had to correct their position, the zigzag path across the lake could almost double the distance. A straight line, while tough to maintain in the wind, was much to be preferred over zigging and zagging their way across the water.

"Want to wait for Lake Agnes for lunch?" Todd asked.

"Okay. Sure."

They studied the map again. They had more than a mile of lake water to cross, and it was sure to be slow going. Then, once into the Nina-Moose River, they faced probably four or five miles of paddling—and a couple of portages—before reaching Lake Agnes.

Todd glanced at his watch. The time was almost eleven o'clock. "It'll be a late lunch."

"That's okay."

"We can eat as soon as we reach Lake Agnes, and then take our time picking out a campsite."

"Right."

As they got to their feet, both of them stared across the choppy waters of Nina-Moose Lake in the direction of the forested tip of the peninsula. They stopped when they heard the dull, droning sound of a motor in the distance.

"Is that a motorboat?" Todd asked.

"I don't see anything."

"It can't be a motorboat—not in here."

"There—an airplane."

The pontoon plane, white with green trim, came over the trees, swerved toward Todd and Mike, and swooped low over them.

"Must be looking for something—or somebody," Todd said.

When the plane dipped down and passed over them, they waved. The plane roared away and disappeared behind trees.

It was early afternoon, and the sun was high in the sky to their left, when they paddled out of Nina-Moose River into Lake Agnes. The wind had died down in the midday heat, and the lake's surface was smooth and shimmery.

Without a word, Todd and Mike pulled their paddles out of the water and rested them on the gunwales as the canoe coasted out into the lake. They both took deep breaths as they looked at the waters of Lake Agnes spread out before them. Breakfast had been a long time ago. They were ready for lunch.

All around the lake there was nothing but woods and quiet. The lake was empty of people. Probably other canoeists would be coming through, some to camp for the night, but for now Lake Agnes belonged to them alone. It felt good.

"Pretty, huh?" Todd said, looking at the tall trees rising around the sparkling water.

"It'll seem prettier after lunch."

"Yeah."

They paddled to the left, along the bank, until they came upon a small clearing that opened from the lake into the woods.

"Okay?"

"Okay."

They turned in. At the bank, Mike leaped out of the bow and pulled the canoe several feet ashore. Todd stepped out of the stern, up to his knees in water, and helped shove the canoe the rest of the way onto the bank.

The clearing was a pleasant patch of land nestled in a cove of woods—good for a midday meal but far from suitable as an overnight campsite. The woods blocked the breeze that would blow away the evening swarms of black flies and mosquitoes. For overnight camping, they wanted a point sticking out into the lake.

Todd reached into one of the large packs and pulled out a brown paper bag marked L–1—the first day's lunch. He emptied the ingredients on a ground cloth—a plastic envelope of peanut butter, bread, dried meat, a pair of apples, a package of Kool-Aid. The menu was designed to avoid cooking at noon. Todd and Mike had learned on their first trip that noontime cooking, whether on the canoe stove or over a campfire, took too much time. They always cooked their breakfast and their dinner. But never lunch.

By the time they had finished eating and were stuffing the wrappings and scraps into the paper bag so they could be burned in the evening campfire, Todd's watch showed the time to be almost two-thirty.

"That point up there—the one with the flat rock, see? —looks perfect for a campsite," Todd said. "What do you say?"

"Right. And we can dip our lines and see about catching dinner, and then have some time for exploring. We've got to pick some blueberries, remember."

"Yeah."

The campsite was set and the midafternoon sun was dipping in the west, behind Todd and Mike. The orange tent with the purple fly was pitched on level ground to one side of the point, a dozen yards back from the water's edge, the door zipped shut against the bugs. A circle of rocks and a stack of wood, in the lee of a huge boulder, awaited the evening's campfire. The food pack dangled at the end of a rope over a high tree limb, out of reach of any foraging animal. The canoe rested on its side at the water's edge, the gear pack underneath it in case of rain. In the water at the bank, drifting easily to and fro, three northern pike, eight to ten inches long, waited on the stringer for the skillet. Todd's first wetting of the flies had produced quick results. Mike had had no luck.

"Want to see what's up that way?" Todd asked, pointing to a path leading up the hill behind the campsite. The path had all the marks of a route to the water for animals —perhaps deer, moose, bear. The animals made their treks to the water's edge at dawn and dusk. Perhaps the signs of alien life—the tent, the canoe, the campers themselves—would deter them. They might choose another route to the water to avoid the threat of the campers. But with the animals' possible arrivals in mind, Todd and Mike had set up the tent to the side of the point, away from what seemed the natural route to the water.

"Yeah, let's go. We've got plenty of time."

With their late lunch, they wouldn't need to think about dinner until dark, so they headed up the hill into the woods, Todd carrying a can for blueberries.

THE WOODS
The Man

The sun was in the west, sending its full glare into the man's face, when, without a sound, a canoe glided through the opening in the opposite bank. The man squinted at it. As the canoe turned to head across the lake, he saw the outline of two figures paddling. He got to his feet, grinning. He had been waiting—how long?—seven or eight hours. It had been a long wait. But seven or eight hours was better than finally having to give up on this lake and locate another one with perhaps more traffic.

The canoe was out onto the lake now, heading in a southerly direction.

For a brief moment, squinting into the sunlight at the canoe, the man wondered if the paddlers might be rangers, dispatched to search the woods for a man who had parachuted out of a 727 jetliner with three-quarters of a million dollars of hijacker loot in canvas bags. But no, of course not. The man shrugged off the fear. There were not enough rangers in the whole world to patrol every lake and stream in these woods in search of a man who needed only to step behind a tree to escape their attention.

No, these were not rangers. These were just what he needed—two paddlers who could tell him his location.

The man turned and began walking along the bank, toward the mouth of a small stream where the canoe obviously was headed. He jogged a few steps, then slowed to a walk again. He did not want to appear anxious, desperate—any of the things he really was. He called out —"Hello!"—and saw the paddlers' heads turn toward him. He waved. The canoe veered course and headed toward him. He could see the paddlers clearly—a young woman in the bow and a young man in the stern. They appeared to be in their middle twenties, about his own age, perhaps a couple of years younger. He waved again, and the young man in the canoe waved back.

The man slowed down and then stopped as the canoeists drew near. They were close enough now for him to call out his question, "What's the name of this lake?" But he didn't. He needed more than the one answer. He needed conversation, casual chatter, which would get him his information without arousing suspicion.

"You need help?" the young man called from the stern of the canoe.

"No, no." He gave them an easy smile. "I'm just here enjoying the peace and quiet."

The paddlers, with one stroke, turned the canoe parallel to the bank and slowed it to a standstill in the water.

"Been out long?" the man asked.

"Three days," the woman answered. She was pretty, with short-cropped blonde hair and a tanned face, and she was smiling.

53

Behind her in the canoe, her companion glanced around. His face took on a puzzled expression. No tent in sight. No canoe. Just a man alone standing on the bank without a trace of gear.

"I'm camped on a lake over the hill there," the man said, waving his arm vaguely at the rise in the land behind him. "Just out for a walk."

"Oh," the man in the canoe said. He seemed satisfied, and the look of puzzlement disappeared.

"What lake is this one?" the man asked. He watched the other man's face. He hoped his words had come across as just a bit of small talk among canoe campers who chanced to cross paths. "Do you know the name of this lake?"

"Oyster Lake," the woman said. She was still smiling in a friendly way.

"Ah, yes, that's what I thought."

With a wave from the woman they paddled away, veering their course back toward the mouth of the small stream.

The man stood on the bank and watched them move away. Then he retraced his steps back along the bank to the flat rock projecting out into the water, and sat down. For a moment he stared across the lake. The sun was getting low. There were three, maybe four hours of daylight left. He had no time to waste.

He took the map out of his shirt pocket and spread it out on the rock in front of him. He smoothed out the folds and stared down at it. Somewhere on that three feet by a foot-and-a-half rectangle of paper was Oyster Lake. One of those thousands of spots of blue was the lake he now sat beside.

He leaned over the map and, beginning in the upper left-hand corner, ran his finger down the edge, reading the names of the lakes in a whisper as his finger moved toward the bottom—Lyons Lake, Greer Lake, Duff Lake . . . Salo Lake, Kemp Lake . . . Little Trout Lake, Mukooda Lake.

He frowned as his glance passed over a nameless lake, and then another—small, unidentified bodies of water.

No, no, he told himself. No need to worry. Oyster Lake was sure to be identified on the map. How else could the couple in the canoe have known the name of the lake they were on?

His finger passed over a large X in blue ink. He smiled when he saw the words below the X—Crane Lake. The X marked one of his five stashes—each a complete set of gear with canoe and paddles, tent, sleeping bag, packs, food—dotted across the BWCA.

He remembered the five days he had spent planting them, one each day. He had been a canoeist going in, a backpacker coming out. Not many backpackers traversed the BWCA. It was canoe country. But only once in the five days had he encountered a pair of campers curious enough to compel him to use his story: He was intentionally staying off the well-traveled trails, indulging himself in a backpacking exercise with his compass. The campers accepted the story.

His finger reached the bottom of the map—Wolf Lake, Lost Lake, Little Lake.

He went back to the top of the map and repeated the procedure—Stewart Lake, Fredrickson Lake, Lindgren Lake.

Four more times his finger reached the bottom of the map and returned to the top.

Then he read the words he was seeking—Oyster Lake.

He almost skipped right by it. His mind was becoming dulled by the recitation of the lakes' names. The numbers were overwhelming, and the list of names seemed unending. But then there it was—Green Lake, Rocky Lake, and Oyster Lake.

The man smiled. Unconsciously, he nodded.

He had indeed landed on the United States side of the international boundary—but just barely. He looked at the mileage scale in the upper right-hand corner of the map, then back at Oyster Lake. He was only a half-dozen or so miles from the Canadian border. At the rate the plane was heading northward when he jumped, a delay of only a second or two would have put him down on the Canadian side. Landing on the U.S. side was important since he was going to be moving a heavy load of United States currency. There were going to be people looking, waiting, and watching for him, and that was problem enough. He did not need the risk of a border crossing.

"Lucky, lucky, lucky," the man said to himself. So far, everything was working out perfectly—better even than he had hoped.

He glanced at the area on the map around Oyster Lake —Hustler Lake and Emerald Lake to the west, Lake Agnes to the east.

56

The man was on the eastern bank of Oyster Lake, looking into the late afternoon sun across the water. Behind him, about a mile and a half to the east, lay Lake Agnes. And, only three or four miles farther to the east lay another of the blue X stash marks on the southern shore of Iron Lake. Counting the walk around the northern edge of Lake Agnes, he was only seven, maybe eight miles at the most from a stash. He glanced up at the sun. Three or more hours of daylight remained. Plenty of time. He could walk seven or eight miles, even through trackless woods, in three hours or so. No problem.

"Lucky, lucky, lucky," he repeated aloud.

With his forefinger, he traced a route out of Iron Lake, away from the stash—overland for a mile to the southern tip of Lac La Croix, down into Lake Agnes, a short walk back to Oyster Lake to pick up the money, and then out of Lake Agnes, south on the Nina-Moose River, across Nina-Moose Lake, south on the Moose River, out onto Echo Trail, and—away, out, free, and rich.

The man stood, folded the map, and replaced it in his pocket, then took one last look at the placid waters of Oyster Lake and turned and walked up the rise away from the water, his back to the slowly setting sun.

Near the top of the rise he stopped. He glanced left and right, then walked to his left, into the clearing. He saw the low mound of leaves and loose dirt in the clump of bushes at the edge covering the business suit, the canvas bags containing the money, and the parachute.

The thought of walking away and leaving the money put a frown on the man's face. But there was no other way. He could not afford to stumble upon someone in the woods with nothing but a couple of fifty-pound canvas bags. He was going to have to circle around Lake Agnes and down the shore of Iron Lake in the late afternoon. He was a cinch to encounter campers, if not worse. No, he had to leave the money. There was no other way.

He turned away and pulled out the compass, staring down at the needle. He looked up—due east—in the direction of Lake Agnes a mile and a half across the woods. That was the simplest way—due east to Lake Agnes. Then, when he returned in his canoe with his gear, he would need only to find the same spot on the bank of Lake Agnes and walk due west to make the pickup. He sighted on a tree at the top of the rise and walked toward it.

After about fifteen minutes the man came upon a small creek. He stopped on the creek bank and took out the map. Unfolding it, then folding it back with the section between Oyster Lake and Iron Lake on the outside, he found the creek, unnamed, on the map. It flowed southward into Nina-Moose River. He was about halfway to the western bank of Lake Agnes. He looked up at the sun. It was dropping to the tips of the trees.

To his left he found a pattern of rocks in the creek and stepped on them to cross the water, then headed up the slight rise in the land, keeping the sun to his back and his eyes on the tree that was his next landmark.

At the top he pulled out the compass again. He started to glance down at it, then stopped dead still, not moving a muscle.

There was no mistaking the sound—a human voice.

The sound came from his left, and not far away. He hardly dared move his head to look. His heart was pounding furiously. Instinctively, he squatted.

Then he stood up quickly. "Stupid," he said to himself. "What could be more suspicious?"

He looked in the direction of the sound, but he saw and heard nothing. Were his ears playing tricks on him? Was his imagination running wild?

Then he heard the sound again—a human voice, undoubtedly. It was saying something that the man did not understand.

He saw a movement—the figure of a person moving through the woods.

He realized that the sound of the voice meant there were two persons. Nobody called out at nothing.

He saw the second person, moving along a couple of yards behind the first one. They appeared to be young men, or perhaps teenaged boys.

But who were they? Why was anyone walking here— between two lakes, a half-mile or so from either of them, just off a tiny creek barely floatable? Had a search party located him? Were there more on the other side, and to the front and rear—all closing in on him? Perhaps the people in the plane had spotted him after all, and now the ones on the ground were closing the circle.

No, no, no, that could not be.

Besides, so what? He had nothing incriminating on him. He was fifteen minutes away from the incriminating cache hidden near Oyster Lake. There was nothing to connect him to it. And even if questioned, he had a ready answer: he was ending a day of walking by returning to his gear at Iron Lake. If the questioners did not believe him, they could walk with him to Iron Lake and he would show them his equipment.

The man looked back to his left and saw the two figures clearly—a pair of teenaged boys. They were not looking at him. They seemed to be saying something to each other. He considered giving a wave—a normal gesture in the woods, sure to allay suspicion—but then he thought better of it. No need to chance a face-to-face conversation. Better he remain just a form in the distance, as they were to him.

He took a deep breath, sighted due east on the compass, selected his next landmark—a tree on a distant rise in the land—and resumed walking.

THE WOODS
Todd and Mike

"Did you see the man?" Todd asked.

"Yeah," Mike said. "For a minute, he scared me."

"Scared you? Why?"

Mike grinned. "Well, not so much scared me as startled me. I thought at first it might be a bear. But bears don't wear jeans and khaki shirts. And then I wondered what a man was doing walking around all alone like, you know, so far from the water, and this late in the afternoon."

Todd and Mike fell into step together and walked down the slope, heading toward the creek.

"We're out here, aren't we, so far from the water and this late in the afternoon," Todd replied. "So why shouldn't he be?"

Mike shrugged. "I guess. It's just that he looked sort of funny, like he was startled, or afraid we were going to see him, or something. Did you see him squat down, like he was trying to duck or something so we wouldn't see him?"

"Yeah." Then Todd added, "Well, if he scared you for a minute, we might have scared him for a minute, too."

"Guess so. But, you know, he didn't wave or holler or

anything, like most people do. He just kept going, like he didn't want us to notice him, or something."

"We didn't wave or holler, either," Todd said with a grin.

"Not after he ducked like that," Mike said. "It was just sort of strange."

"Nobody in these woods expects to meet someone else, and I guess it's a little surprising when suddenly there's someone there."

"Uh-huh. Let's follow this creek. It bends to the west right up there. Probably runs into a lake."

Todd glanced ahead at the late-afternoon sun. Two, maybe three hours of daylight remained. They were only about fifteen minutes away from their campsite on Lake Agnes. They had plenty of time. "Sure, let's see," Todd said.

They skipped over the creek, using the same rocks the man had stepped on, and turned to their right, angling toward the bend in the creek that pointed due west.

"Neat little creek," Mike said.

"If you like portaging," Todd said.

"Yeah, enough rocks, that's for sure."

As they walked, occasionally leaving the bank of the creek to raid a blueberry bush, the size and number of the rocks in the creek increased.

"Portage city," Mike said.

"Yeah."

"I can't imagine anyone trying this in a canoe."

"Hey, this looks like a portage path."

They moved over onto the path and, going down a slope, suddenly saw a lake in front of them.

"Wow!" Mike said.

"Pretty, yeah," Todd said. "It's so all alone and quiet."

Todd and Mike stood for a moment and watched the rays of the late-afternoon sun streaming through the trees on the opposite bank and bouncing off the water's surface. Then they walked toward the lake, angling to their left, away from the creek, toward the higher land.

"What lake is it?" Mike asked.

Todd pulled the map from his pocket, and they stopped while he unfolded the map. He found Lake Agnes easily enough, ran his finger to the left, and said, "Must be Oyster Lake."

They walked to the water's edge and then along the bank, in a southerly direction. The mirror surface of the lake was broken only by the fish grabbing for bugs settling on the water at day's end.

"Look at that," Todd said as a fish briefly flashed into view and then disappeared. "I'll bet that even you could catch a fish in this lake." All three of the northern pike on the stringer back at Lake Agnes had been landed by Todd, and he wasn't about to let Mike forget it.

"Okay, okay," Mike said. "Just wait until tomorrow."

They came to a large flat rock extending out into the lake and sat down. Mike tossed a couple of small stones into the lake, and they watched the ripples wrinkle the smooth surface of the water. All was quiet. All was still. "Might be good to bring our stuff over here and stay a couple of nights," Mike said. "Not many people paddling through here, I'll bet."

Todd was tempted to agree. Lake Agnes sometimes was a highway loaded with canoe traffic heading for the interior. "We'll be in Lac La Croix tomorrow, and that'll be okay."

"Yeah."

"Want to head back? The sun is getting down there pretty low."

"Sure. And let's keep an eye out for blueberry bushes."

The boys got to their feet. Mike sailed one more small stone into Oyster Lake for good measure, and then they turned and headed up the rise.

The route back was sure to be no problem. It was simply a matter of keeping the creek on their left until it turned south, then crossing it and picking up the animal path that led down the slope into Lake Agnes.

For the first couple of hundred yards Todd and Mike walked in silence and kept their eyes on the ground, watching their footing. Then, near a clearing at the top of the rise, Todd said, "I'll bet there are some blueberries in that clearing. C'mon."

They veered to their right and stepped into the clearing. It was dotted and edged with blueberry bushes.

"What'd I tell you?" Todd said.

"Looks like an orchard of them."

"Let's get to work and then we'd better head back. The sun is getting low."

They moved together around the edge of the clearing, picking berries and dropping them into the can Todd carried.

"Look at that," Todd said.

They stared down at a small mound of leaves and loose dirt, obviously fresh, in a clump of blueberry bushes.

64

"It looks like a grave," Mike said.

Todd poked at the mound with the toe of his sneaker.

"Don't," Mike said.

"Why not?"

"What if it is a grave—some animal or something?"

"Animals don't bury their dead."

"But there's something funny about it."

The loose dirt fell away and the toe of Todd's sneaker revealed a patch of blue fabric, then a patch of white silk.

"What is it?" Mike asked.

Todd withdrew his foot and bent over. "Looks like clothes or something." He reached down and pulled out the blue suit jacket. "That's what it is—clothes," he said. "Of all things. Who would bury clothes out here in the woods?"

Mike bent over and lifted out a pair of trousers, the dark blue matching the jacket. "This is a business suit," he said. "I can't believe it."

"Let's see what else . . ."

"I wonder who . . . ?"

"That man we saw back there—?"

"Maybe so. But why?"

Todd picked up a white dress shirt. A necktie fell out of it. He dropped the shirt on the ground.

Mike reached in and grabbed the edge of the parachute. "This isn't clothes," he said. He pulled more of the material out from under the clump of bushes, reeling it in with both hands. "It's a—"

They both spoke the word together: "Parachute!"

"Look," Mike said. "It's got a harness and everything."

65

"I never saw a parachute before," Todd said, staring down at the expanse of white silk in his hands.

"Neither did I."

"Somebody parachuted in here," Todd said. He spoke the words slowly, as if he could not believe what he was saying. "Parachuted in—here? And in a business suit?"

"Uh-huh."

"It doesn't make sense."

"Sure doesn't."

"What's this?" Todd dropped the parachute and scraped away some loose dirt. He reached in and picked up a khaki canvas bag. "It's heavy," he said. "Something's in it."

"There's another one," Mike said. "Weird-looking packs."

"I don't think they're packs. Just canvas bags with straps. I never saw anything like it."

"Me, either."

Todd knelt, placed the bag on the ground, and felt around for snaps or a zipper or a buckle.

"Are you going to open it?"

"Why not?"

"Well, it's just—"

"Somebody's left this stuff behind—and recently, too. Look at it. It hasn't been rained on. I'll bet it hasn't been here more than a few hours."

"That man we passed back there," Mike said again.

"Yeah. Let's see what he left behind."

Todd popped loose a row of snaps and peeled back a flap to reveal a heavy-duty zipper. He unzipped the lid of the bag, lifted it, and looked in. Mike leaned forward and looked over Todd's shoulder.

They stared down at stacks of currency—twenty-dollar bills—bound with white tape in half-inch-thick decks.

"Holy cow!" Todd said.

Mike exhaled with a low whistling sound.

Agent Stoneham

The television crews and the newspaper reporters had left the back room at Barney's, heading for telephones to file their stories. They had precious little to report. Ted Stoneham, bowing to the increasing clamor for interviews with each new arrival of reporters during the day, finally agreed to a news conference. He explained what the agents, rangers, troopers, and deputies were doing. Then he answered questions, usually with one word: no. Were there any leads? No. Were there any clues as to the hijacker's identity? No. Any sign of the hijacker at all? No. Has the parachute been found? No. Do you know which side of the border he landed on? No. And so it went—no, no, no—until the television crews and the newspaper reporters finally went away.

Stoneham, alone now, circled the room slowly. He stopped when he came to the array of maps pinned to the wall, stared at them, and frowned. There were so many —so very many—acres of wilderness, and so many—so very many—lakes and streams. There were so many people out there. And somewhere out there, on one of those acres of wilderness, perhaps by now paddling on one of those hundreds of lakes and streams, was a hijacker with three-quarters of a million dollars of loot. But which acre of wilderness? Which lake or stream? And which person, of the hundreds or so? The campers were coming to the end of the day, dragging their canoes onto the bank, setting up their tents, building their campfires. But which lakeshore, which tent, which campfire harbored a hijacker? Maybe none of them. Maybe he already had made good his getaway. Maybe the state troopers and the sheriff's deputies and the rangers were ringing an area the hijacker already had left behind.

The setting sun was visible through the window. The first day of the search was coming to an end. And Ted Stoneham had nothing—no clue at all. The spotters in the small planes and helicopters had reported nothing unusual. But then, how could they? Unless the man spread out a huge banner—"I am the hijacker"—there was no way to identify him. Officers were manning the major takeout points and the arteries of blacktop and dirt roads leading to them, but it was impossible to intercept and question everyone coming out. There were too many takeout points. At last report, they had questioned about sixty canoeists. But again—nothing unusual. The net result of it all: nothing.

Stoneham shifted his stance in front of the large map displaying the entire BWCA. He looked at the jagged line indicating the border between the United States and Canada. Then his eyes traced a straight penciled line extending from the southwest corner of the BWCA on a north-northeasterly trajectory. It was the line of flight of the jet carrying the hijacker. Where the border and the flight trajectory intersected—a place called Painted Rock on Lac La Croix—concentric circles spread out like ripples on a pond. The center of the circles was, the pilot of the jet said, approximately where the hijacker bailed out. He had to come to land somewhere inside the larger of the circles. But where? Inside the United States or inside Canada? It could be either.

The Canadians were being helpful, as always, sending Mounties to work with rangers in fanning out through the area. But like Stoneham's own officers, their reports added up to—nothing.

So many acres, so many lakes, so many streams—and a man nobody knew.

Stoneham turned away from the map. Neither the penciled marking of the jet's flight path nor the concentric circles indicating the hijacker's landing spot really mattered now. The parachutist had hit the ground almost eighteen hours ago. He might be anywhere by this time.

And with the passage of time, the dim hope faded that a camper in all those acres of wilderness would report having seen the parachute in the moonlight, heard the landing, encountered a stranger dropping out of the sky.

The telephone on the table rang, and he walked across and lifted the receiver. "Stoneham here."

The familiar voice of Joe Snider came through the line from the FBI office in Minneapolis. "Ted, maybe we've got something."

"What?"

"The stewardess—Gloria Marsh."

"Yes. Did she make a fix?"

"Maybe so, maybe not—probably maybe so."

Stoneham sighed. "Mind telling me what that means?" he said.

"We may have a fix, but nobody—including Miss Marsh—can be absolutely certain."

"Tell me."

"Well, we went on the assumption that our man had to know something—I mean, a lot—about parachuting. And he had to know something about the wiring system of an airplane—only way he could bypass the lock on the door in flight. And we had her description—probably blond or reddish hair, clean-shaven, slim, and probably from east Texas because he talks that way."

"Yeah."

"All those factors left us with a very short list."

"But a list of possibilities."

"Yeah, a list of sorts. So we got together a set of mug shots—some of them our own agents, you know, just to muddy the waters—and showed them to Miss Marsh."

"And?"

"She picked one of the real prospects—not one of our agents, you know—and she seems pretty certain, but I don't know—"

"Don't know what?"

"Well, all she can identify, she says, are the eyes."

Stoneham was silent a moment. He remembered Gloria Marsh's claim that she would recognize the man's eyes. Perhaps she had been able to make good on her

71

promise. "I think that's good," Stoneham said. "The eyes are probably the only genuine part of him that she saw."

"Maybe so."

"Whose eyes are they?"

"They belong to one Byron Matthews, twenty-eight years of age, a former paratrooper. Discharged a couple of years ago. Worked for a while as a mechanic for American Airlines in Tulsa, and then pretty much dropped out of sight. And—"

"And what?"

"He's from Palestine, Texas, which pleased Miss Marsh. That's just south of Marshall, Texas. She picked the guy with the right accent."

"Okay."

"There's more."

"What?"

"When he quit the paratroopers, and again later when he quit American Airlines, he told friends he was going to see the country—fish the streams and travel the paths, is the way he put it."

"And nobody's seen him since?"

"Not that we know of, except for a couple of postcards to friends—one from Alaska about six months ago, and— get this—one from Ely, Minnesota, about three months ago."

"That's interesting. Any criminal record?"

"Not that we can find."

"Anything else?"

"That's about it. Anything happening at your end?"

"The sun is setting," Stoneham said flatly. "That's about all."

72

Snider chuckled. "Talk to you later."

"Sure."

Stoneham replaced the telephone in its cradle. He pulled a yellow pad in front of him, picked up a pencil, and wrote: "Our man may be one Byron Matthews, age twenty-eight, former paratrooper, former American Airlines employee, no known criminal record, indications he visited BWCA three months ago, hometown Palestine, Texas."

He tore the sheet off the pad and walked through the restaurant, out the front door, and across the street to the sheriff's office. "Can you radio this to the troopers and deputies in the area?" he asked the young woman at the desk.

"Sure," she said. She glanced at the handwritten notes and looked up at Stoneham. "How'd you get him identified so quickly?"

Stoneham managed a half grin at the young woman's friendly question. The identification had not come quickly at all. Eighteen hours was not to be considered fast work. And besides, quick or slow, they had no way of knowing for sure they were right with the identification. Byron Matthews, age twenty-eight, might turn up selling used cars in Los Angeles. But the lead was all they had. And if correct, there always was the chance that the hijacker, unaware his identity was known, would play it straight at a roadblock and blithely offer up his driver's license—with the name Byron Matthews—in response to an officer's request. Smaller strokes of good fortune had broken larger cases than this one.

"We can't be absolutely certain he's the one," Stone-

73

ham said, "but it looks like a pretty good maybe."

He walked back out into the fading light and crossed the street to Barney's Restaurant.

"How about a hamburger," he asked Barney, "when you get a chance."

"Comin' up."

Stoneham walked back into the back room.

THE WOODS
Todd and Mike

"The hijacker," Mike said softly.

"Sure."

They were kneeling over one of the canvas bags, the flap turned back, staring down at the packets of currency.

The other bag, off to the side, was open, showing more stacks of money.

"Just look at it all," Mike said. "I wonder how much there is."

"The radio said he was demanding three-quarters of a million dollars. And I guess that's how much he got."

Mike whistled softly. "I never saw so much money all at one time."

"Me, either."

"He bailed out of an airplane with the money!" Mike's voice carried a tone of awe. "He parachuted into the woods at night—wow!"

"Yeah, and that explains the pontoon plane. They know he bailed out somewhere around here and that he's in these woods. They're out looking for him."

"Him," Mike repeated.

They looked at each other.

"Do you think it's the man we passed back there?" Mike asked.

"Must be," Todd said.

Unconsciously, both of them glanced around, as if the man might be returning and closing in on them at that moment.

"But why—why would he leave the money here?" Mike asked.

"He'll be coming back for it," Todd answered.

"But I don't get it. He got the money and he got away. He bailed out, landed safely—and then he goes off and leaves the money under a bush. It just doesn't make sense."

"Yeah, I think it does," Todd said slowly. "He'll be back. He's gone to pick up the gear to get him out of here —a canoe, a tent, you know—so he'll look just like anyone else moving around in here. He couldn't afford to go walking through the woods carrying two bags of money and nothing else—not with the police and everybody looking for him."

"I guess, but—"

"Yeah," Todd said with a smile, "he took a big gamble that nobody would stumble across the money—and it looks like he lost."

Todd picked up one of the packets of currency and hefted it in his hand.

"Are they all twenties?" Mike asked.

Todd thumbed through the stack of bills. "Looks like it."

76

"Wow!"

"Wait a minute—*shhh!*"

"What?" Mike whispered.

Todd held up a hand to silence Mike. "Wait. Maybe I'm hearing things, but . . ." He turned slowly and surveyed the woods behind them. He saw the trees, the bushes, the sky—and nothing else. He listened to the sounds of the woods. He heard the gentle murmur of leaves moving in a soft breeze. He heard the flutter of birds taking flight. But he heard nothing else—no crackling sound of a man walking through untracked woods.

"Do you think he's coming back?" Mike asked in a whisper.

"He might. He saw us. I'm sure of it. He knew which way we were heading."

"Yeah," Mike said slowly. He was glancing around. "Remember how he ducked down like he didn't want us to see him?"

"Uh-huh," Todd said. "And what worries me is that he knows we saw him trying to duck us—sort of suspicious for somebody in canoe country, wouldn't you say?—and he knows that, too." He paused. "I know that if I had left three-quarters of a million dollars hidden in the woods and spotted a couple of people heading toward it, I'd sure come back."

"We'd better get out of here."

"I think so, too."

"Which way? We'll walk right into him if we go back that way."

"Not if we're careful."

They both looked down at the currency stacked neatly

in the canvas bag. Then they looked at each other. Neither spoke.

Finally Todd said, "Let's stuff all these things back under the bushes—back like it was—and toss some dirt and leaves on top."

"Huh?"

"That way, if the man comes back he won't know—at least not right off—that somebody has found his stuff."

Todd began gathering up the waves of white silk, then picked up the suit, knelt, and shoved the mass under the clump of bushes.

Mike zipped and snapped the money bags. "What about the money?" he asked.

Todd glanced at Mike, and before he could reply the silence of the woods was broken by the *whack-whack-whack* sound of a helicopter. Todd and Mike looked up, scanning the sky. The helicopter came at them over the trees, nose down, flying low. A face peered out of its window. Todd and Mike watched as the helicopter roared over them and vanished from sight as quickly as it had appeared.

Neither of them said anything for a moment. Mike's question—"What about the money?"—still hung in the air, unanswered.

"Do you think they saw us?" Mike asked finally.

"How could they miss?"

"Do you think they'll come back?"

"I don't think so. They're not looking for a couple of teenagers. They saw us, and they went on. They won't be back."

"Maybe we should have waved them down."

"It all happened so fast," Todd said. "Let's get out of here."

"The money . . . ?"

"Let's take it back to camp," Todd said. "We can figure out what to do from there."

"Do you think we should?"

"We can't just leave it here."

Mike nodded. "I guess."

"Wait a minute," Todd said.

"What?"

"First let's make sure the man's not coming back."

"Yeah."

Todd picked up the money bags and tossed them under the bush. "If we meet up with him, we'll just wave and keep going," he said. "Nothing out of the ordinary. Right?"

"Right."

Together they trekked to the top of the rise and peered out into the woods. There was no movement, no sound, no sign of life. The man was gone, and there were no indications he was doubling back. They returned to the money.

"Okay," Todd said, hoisting one of the bags and draping the strap over his shoulder. "Now we've got to be careful that we don't run into him—either meeting him on his way back or overtaking him on his way out."

"It would be kind of awkward, wouldn't it?" Mike said with a nervous smile as he lifted the other bag and slipped his arm through the strap.

Wordlessly and slowly, they began walking back up the rise, away from Oyster Lake, toward their campsite at Lake Agnes. At the top of each rise they stopped and stared at the woods spread out before them, looking for any sign of human life, any movement. They saw nothing.

After twenty minutes of walking they turned right with the stream and, after ten more minutes, came upon the trail leading to Lake Agnes.

"Hold it a minute," Todd said softly.

Mike stopped.

"If he's laying for us, this is where he will be doing it."

Mike stared down the path until his line of sight ended with a bend. All appeared quiet, peaceful, harmless.

"Back there in the woods, he had no way of knowing where we were going to be coming from—no path, you know, and no way to predict where we were going to be. But here it's different—on a path."

"Uh-huh. You're right. We'd better stay off the path."

"Yeah, I think so. It'll be a little slower but a lot safer."

They left the path behind and followed the stream south for another fifty yards. Then they turned left. Moving parallel to the path, they struck out through the woods.

"This way, at least we can hear him coming—or see him," Todd said. Then he added, "If he's even around here."

Mike nodded.

Behind them, the sun was low in the sky. The trees cast lengthened shadows.

"This stuff is heavy," Mike whispered with a grin.

"Yeah. Imagine parachuting with these things hanging on you."

"Maybe he figured that being rich was worth it."

Todd glanced across at Mike and said nothing.

They pushed through the woods and onto the shore of Lake Agnes in fifteen minutes.

To their left, about fifty yards up the bank, they saw their orange tent on the point with the red canoe pulled ashore. Nothing had been moved. All appeared normal.

They stood on the bank for a moment. There were no canoes on the lake. The hour of canoe travel had passed. The campers scattered throughout the BWCA were setting up their tents, gathering firewood, beginning their supper preparations in the fading light. Other campers were probably somewhere along the shoreline, but Todd and Mike saw nobody. If people were there, their campfires would identify them later.

Todd took a deep breath and exhaled. "I think we've made it," he said.

"Let's get to the campsite," Mike said.

They picked their way along the fifty yards of shoreline to their camp.

"Let's get this stuff into the tent," Todd said.

THE WOODS
The Man

The sun was down and the only light was a purplish haze —still bright enough to see by but fading fast—when the man arrived at the shore of the lake.

He stopped short of the bank and looked around the shoreline. There were no campfires or tents in sight. He scanned the quiet surface of the water. There were no canoes on the lake.

He walked down to the water's edge and took his map out of his shirt pocket. Squinting in the dying light, he stared at the section folded out.

This had to be Iron Lake. He had skirted the top of Lake Agnes and moved down the eastern bank to a portage path, then had struck out due east again. His progress took him to an unnamed lake, which confirmed he was on the right track. He moved around the northern edge of the small lake and resumed his movement due east. This had to be Iron Lake.

Without further hesitation, and still holding the folded map in his right hand, he headed to his right, southward, along the bank, toward the lower tip of Iron Lake. He walked briskly, jogging when the terrain allowed. The light was fading. He had to hurry. He must find the stash before darkness fell.

Less than three hundred yards along the bank, he spotted a dark green canoe in the bushes ahead. He smiled and quickened his pace.

Reaching the canoe, he righted it, uncovering a large pack and a pair of paddles. He glanced up into the purple sky. The food pack, undisturbed, dangled at the end of a rope over a high branch.

"Okay," the man said aloud. "All right."

The stars were flung out across the velvety black of the sky. Just above the cloudless horizon, the moon, still full, was coming up. Below the moon and stars and the black sky, the man sat cross-legged on a ground cloth in front of a small crackling campfire. He sipped coffee from a thermos mug and stared into the dark distance across the lake. Behind him stood a green pop-up tent, and to the left of the tent the canoe was a dark shadow in the moonlight.

The man sighed and took another sip of the coffee. The hot liquid tasted good in the chill of the evening. He was on the home stretch: The danger of taking the airplane hostage on the ground with its crew and passengers had passed. The danger of waiting for the airline's decision about whether or not they were going to pay the money had passed. The danger of the takeoff—maybe a trick of some sort by the pilot—had passed. The danger of the pilot getting the smart idea of changing routes in the air had passed. The danger of the jump had passed. He had landed safely. He had separated himself from any evidence—including the money—that might link him to the hijacking. He was safe, sitting before a campfire next to his tent, sipping coffee and staring into the darkness.

One more risk, that was all: picking up the money and getting out of the woods.

He wondered absently if the FBI had succeeded in identifying him. Probably not. He decided that that stewardess had not been fooled by the blackened hair and beard. He had seen the realization in her eyes. But, still, what could she say? The hair was dyed. So what? She still did not know the real color. And he knew that the bulky blue suit over the camping clothes gave an impression of a stockier man. It was strange the way she had stared into his eyes, though, as if trying to memorize every fleck of color. Well, okay, so she knew that the hijacker was blue eyed. The police were hardly going to arrest every blue-eyed camper coming out of the woods. Still, an identification was something to avoid when coming out of the woods. He unconsciously reached back and felt the wallet in his hip pocket. He probably was safe enough, but he made a mental note to scrupulously avoid any action that might prompt an officer to ask for identification.

The man smiled slightly and felt himself relax. There was no risk involved in sleeping on the southern shore of Iron Lake. He was a canoe camper. That was all. Who was to say anything else?

There wasn't any risk in returning to the money tomorrow morning, either. The route was simple and—luckily—short. He needed to paddle about a mile and a half north along the western shore of Iron Lake. From there, a mile's portage led into the southern tip of Lac La Croix. The man remembered the ranger's cabin marked on the map at the point where he would enter Lac La Croix. It might be fun to stop in and say hello. What could be more innocent in appearance? But no; he decided the hour was going to be a little too early for casual visiting and might indeed arouse suspicion, especially for a man alone. Most campers were not out and moving on the lakes at daybreak. No, he would glide quietly past the ranger's cabin. From there, he needed only to paddle across the tip of Lac La Croix, make one short portage, and move down into Lake Agnes. A couple of miles down the western bank of Lake Agnes was going to bring him to the place where he needed to bank the canoe and take a walk, due west, to Oyster Lake.

The man frowned when he thought of the spot where he needed to come out of Lake Agnes. He remembered the campsite—the orange tent with the purple fly, the red canoe pulled ashore, the food pack hanging from a high tree limb—just to the north of where he had to strike out through the woods. Coming out yesterday, he had spotted the orange tent in plenty of time to circle around it. He hadn't seen anybody around the campsite and decided it belonged to the two boys he saw near Oyster Lake. Perhaps they would still be camped there in the morning. He hoped not. But even more than that, he hoped the boys had returned to their campsite without going all the way to Oyster Lake. What if they happened—just happened—to spot the mound of loose dirt, and poke around

85

in it? What if they unearthed a couple of canvas bags? They were sure to investigate. And then—what?

The thought troubled the man, and his frown deepened. But he told himself again that he was smart to leave the money bags behind. Oh, sure, now that he had made his way safely to the stash without encountering anyone, it would have been good to have brought the money with him. But the bags were a suspicious burden for a man out for a stroll in the woods. No, he was wise to leave them and pick them up later when they fitted in nicely with all the other gear. The chances of the money being found buried in a clump of bushes deep back inside the woods were a million to one.

"Well," the man said aloud, "maybe not quite a million to one," and he smiled, "but pretty close to it."

But later, with the campfire doused, he lay inside the tent in the dark comfort of the sleeping bag, eyes wide open, and wondered about the two teenaged boys he had seen heading for the shore of Oyster Lake.

THE WOODS
Todd and Mike

They were seated next to each other in front of a low campfire. Todd was hugging his knees and staring into the fire. Mike was leaning back on one hand, gazing past the fire into the darkness. The full moon was high in the sky. The moonbeams cast a ghostly gray-white coating over the trees and the ground, and splashed a glittering silver surface across the still waters of Lake Agnes. On the campfire, a metal pot rested on two small logs. The water inside, while not up to boiling, gave off a slight vapor of steam.

"Maybe we should have just left the money there," Todd said.

Mike said nothing.

"We could have flagged down that helicopter," Todd continued. "I guess we should have."

"It passed over too quickly. It all happened too fast. You said so yourself. It was gone before we knew it was there."

Todd nodded without speaking. Neither he nor Mike had mentioned the money since placing the two canvas bags in the tent more than four hours earlier. They had built their dinner campfire, filleted the three northern pike, melted shortening in the skillet, rolled the fish in cornmeal, cooked, eaten, and cleaned up—all the while with a strained sort of chatter that avoided any mention of the stacks of twenty-dollar bills packed into canvas bags in their tent. It was as if each wanted the other to make the first mention—to set the tone for a discussion of the question at hand: what to do now?

Todd leaned forward, picked up a stick, and poked the fire gently with it. The flames licked up a little higher around the pot of water. "Maybe we should have headed for a takeout point with the money and turned it in. We probably had enough daylight to make it." He paused. "That's what we'll do in the morning, first thing," he said finally.

Mike shifted his position on the ground and leaned forward, staring into the fire. Without turning toward Todd he said, "You know, we might not have to turn the money in."

The words seemed to hang in the air for a full minute.

"You mean, keep the money?"

"Yes."

Todd laughed softly.

"What's so funny?"

"What you just said."

"What's funny about that?"

"It's what I've been thinking, too. But I was waiting for you to be the one to say it."

"Okay, I said it."

"It was in both our minds when the helicopter went over, so we just stood there like a couple of statues without trying to wave it down."

"Well, what do you think?"

"I'll admit I've been thinking about it."

"And—?"

Todd poked the fire again. He took a deep breath. "It just wouldn't be right to keep the money."

"What's so wrong about it?"

Todd dropped the stick on the fire, and the end blazed. "It's stolen money," he said. "It's not ours."

Mike leaned forward and wrapped his arms around his knees. He turned toward Todd. "Look, I've been doing some thinking, too, and—"

"I know, I know," Todd said. "It's a lot of money."

"It sure is."

"But it's not ours."

"Listen to me a minute, will you?"

"Sure. Go ahead."

"Whose money is it? It's the hijacker's. I mean, he had possession of it. He had it, and we found it. And you know what? If we hadn't stumbled on it, he would have come back and picked it up, made his getaway and lived happily ever after in Acapulco or some place. The airline, or the insurance company, or whatever, was going to be out the money, right? So this way, they're not out the money any more than if we hadn't found it. Our finding it is no different than the hijacker having it, as far as they're concerned, right?"

"Good grief!" Todd said. "I hope that when you get

to Iowa State you'll take a course in logic or ethics or something. The professor will be fascinated by your line of reasoning."

"College is what I'm talking about," Mike said. "Neither of us is a little rich boy. My dad's already made it clear that he's paying for some things not covered by the football scholarship—and I've got to pay for everything else. That means I've got to get a job in the off-season. You're even worse off. You won't have a football scholarship to help you. You ought to be making this argument —not me."

Todd was silent.

"With this money—"

"I know," Todd said.

"With this money," Mike repeated, "we'd sail through —a car, plenty of clothes, spending money, no part-time jobs. Don't you see?"

"Sure I see."

"Well, then?"

"It's still not right. It's not our money."

Mike sighed.

"Look," Todd said, "there are two bags of money. If you want to do it, take one of the bags, and we'll turn in the other one and tell them that we just found one bag."

Mike, hugging his knees, kept his gaze on the small orange flames of the campfire.

"I won't tell on you, if that's what's worrying you."

"It's not that," Mike said.

"Well, what?"

Mike turned to Todd. He had a small smile on his face.

"I can't do it—any more than you can," he said. "But I'll admit I was sort of hoping you'd talk me into it. After all, you're the realist in the group."

"It's a lot of money," Todd said.

"It sure is."

"You know, don't you," Todd said with a grin, "that I've just saved you from being arrested on the football practice field at Iowa State when the police discovered that the bills you're throwing around had the same numbers as the bills turned over to the hijacker."

"Wow! I never thought of that," Mike said. "Say, is that why you—"

Todd let the question go by. He said only, "But it sure is a lot of money."

HEADQUARTERS
Agent Stoneham

Ted Stoneham looked at his wristwatch. Almost ten o'-clock.

The changing of the shift was coming up. All the FBI agents, state troopers, rangers, and sheriff's deputies who were on duty since morning would be checking in before going off duty. They would be stopping in to report the bits and pieces of information they had picked up—or the lack of information.

Stoneham knew that bits and pieces were the most he could hope for. Anything significant would have been radioed in to the sheriff's office for relay to him immediately. And there had not been one radio report from the field.

He walked to the door. "Barney," he called out. "Have we got enough coffee for all the men coming in?"

Barney grinned from behind the counter. A customer seated there munching a hamburger turned and looked at Stoneham with open curiosity. Barney said, "Sure, don't worry."

When the first of the officers began arriving, Stoneham

could not help comparing them. Each of the groups seemed to be a type all its own. His own FBI agents looked like young suburbanites heading into a vacation trip to the north woods—clean shaven, neatly trimmed hair, fair skin for the most part, and a newish look to their jeans and denim shirts. The state troopers were lean, erect, well groomed, immaculate in their pressed uniforms, even after a day in the field. The rangers were a tanned, sinewy bunch. Like Lars Nillsen, they all wore the permanent squint around the eyes of men who spend their lives outside in the wind and the sunshine. Their uniforms, designed more for endurance than appearance, all seemed to have endured a lot. The deputies, wearing anything from khaki trousers and a T-shirt to jeans and a faded sports shirt, had open, relaxed faces—neither the blank expression of the FBI agents nor the stern countenance of the state troopers nor the leathery skin of the rangers.

Stoneham took a seat at the head of the long table and leaned back, waiting. Several times he called out to a new group entering, "Coffee's out there, if you want it." And finally he asked, "Everyone here?"

The last arrivals were bringing their coffee mugs to the table and sitting down.

"Everybody got the ID and the description?" he asked. The men seated along the two sides of the long table nodded and mumbled their yeses. "And all of you passed the information along to your relief?" Again, nods and mumbled yeses.

"I assume, since we haven't heard anything from you

from the field, that none of you encountered anything resembling our man, or any trace of him."

For a moment nobody moved or spoke. Then a deputy sheriff at the far end of the table raised his right hand slightly for attention and asked, "Didn't you get my message?"

"What message?"

"About the couple coming out who said they ran into a man alone asking where he was? We talked this morning about—"

Stoneham frowned. "No, I didn't get the message. What have you got?"

"I radioed in a couple of hours ago," the deputy said, a look of puzzlement on his face. "Didn't Sara—?"

Stoneham sighed. In his mind he saw the girl operating the radio in the sheriff's office across the street. He also saw in his mind a note on the table in front of her, awaiting his arrival to inquire about messages. Sara had seen no urgency in the message. Or perhaps she had been told not to leave the radio.

"You talked to some people who ran into a man who didn't know where he was," Stoneham repeated flatly. "All right, go on. What else?"

"They were coming out at dusk—at Meander Lake—and we had a lot of people coming out all along there about that time, and they were backed up waiting for us to question everyone. They were pretty nearly the last ones, and—"

"What did they say?"

"Well, in the middle of the afternoon, going across

Oyster Lake, a man on the bank hailed them, and they paddled over and visited with him a couple of minutes. In the course of the conversation, the man said he was camped on another lake and was just out for a walk, and had come upon this lake and wondered what the name of the lake was, and they told him—Oyster Lake. They thought it was kind of odd that he wouldn't know where he was and would be so casual about it."

"Oyster Lake," Stoneham repeated. "Anything else?"

"Just that I asked if he had a canoe and they said, no, they didn't see one." The deputy paused. "Look, I radioed that information in to Sara and told her that you might need it."

"It's okay," Stoneham said. "Did they give you any description of the man?"

"Not much. Reddish blond hair. Clean shaven. Clothes pretty clean, too, as if he hadn't been in the woods for long."

"Short or tall? Fat or skinny? How old?"

The deputy looked down at a notebook. "Five feet ten, maybe eleven, inches tall. Sturdy, muscular build, maybe a hundred and seventy pounds. Late twenties or maybe thirty years old." He looked up from the notebook. "No noticeable scars or anything like that."

"Uh-huh." Stoneham got to his feet and gestured for Lars Nillsen to join him at the map. "Where's Oyster Lake?"

Without hesitation, Nillsen placed the end of a forefinger on a small circle of blue in the western section of the BWCA—a point within the large red circle marking the area where the pilot guessed the hijacker would have landed.

Stoneham turned back to the men at the table. "Have we got people on the way in there?"

Nobody replied.

Stoneham looked at the sheriff, then at the ranking state trooper.

Finally Nillsen spoke. "Not really much point at this stage. The man didn't hang around Oyster Lake for ten minutes after finding out his location. You can bet on it. He headed straight for the nearest stash—and no telling where that might be."

"I guess so," Stoneham said. He and Nillsen sat back down. "Anyone else send a message that I didn't receive?" he asked with a tone of exasperation.

"I didn't send a message," came a voice from Stoneham's right, halfway down the long table. The speaker was clearly a ranger. Stoneham did not remember his face from the morning meeting. He probably was one of those who came from a post in the woods during the day to join the force manning the takeout points. "But Lars mentioned a stash, and I heard about something that might mean something."

"What?"

"The Canadians told me that a couple of canoeists reported finding some lost gear. That's what they called it—lost gear."

"Lost gear . . . ?" Stoneham was puzzled. Then he asked, "The Canadians? What Canadians?"

"The customs people over at Prairie Portage."

"What's that about lost gear? I don't understand."

"Well, the canoeists told the Canadian customs people that they had come upon some gear that seemed to have been left behind—lost or something."

Stoneham waited.

"It was stashed," the ranger said. "A canoe, overturned, with a pack full of utensils, a sleeping bag, and a tent, all rolled up, and a food pack tied high up in a tree."

Somebody on the other side of the table said, "Aw, c'mon, you know that lots of people leave their campsites —their gear—for fishing, or exploring, or whatever."

"Yes, yes. But they said this gear had been out there in the woods for quite some time. It had been rained on, and it was dirty. It hadn't been touched in a long time." He paused, "And then when Lars said that maybe the hijacker was heading for a stash—some gear he had stashed in the woods a while back—well . . ."

"Right," Stoneham said. "Where was this stash?"

"Snowbank Lake."

"That's a mighty long walk from Oyster Lake," Nillsen said.

"Where is it?"

Nillsen got up and pointed to a spot in the southeastern section of the BWCA. Stoneham watched without getting up, then turned back to the ranger. "When did they spot this stash?"

"Yesterday."

Nillsen sat back down. "If I were the hijacker," he said, "I'd have had more than one stash. This stash may be one of his, but I'll bet it's not the one he's heading for. I'll bet there's another one, which is closer to Oyster Lake."

Stoneham nodded slowly.

"We ought to get someone out there right away," Nillsen said to Stoneham.

"If you're so sure that this one isn't the one that he's heading for—"

"We need to count the paddles."

"Count the paddles?"

"Experienced canoeists always take along a spare paddle. Nothing worse than breaking a paddle deep in the woods, in the middle of a trip, and not having a spare to use. If there are two paddles in that stash, our man is operating alone, and you can bet on it. But if there are three paddles—well, then, we're looking for a pair of people coming out. That's worth knowing, isn't it?"

Stoneham watched Lars Nillsen with admiration. The man not only knew the woods, he knew how to make his brain function. "Can we get somebody in there tonight?"

"Sure. No problem—a short trip and a moonlit night." Nillsen looked down the table. "Luke, you know the area. Why don't you go in with Fred?"

"Sure," said the ranger named Luke.

Nillsen looked at Fred, the ranger who had reported the sighting of the stash. "Did they say where on Snowbank Lake? It's a big lake."

"Northern shore, that's all."

"You want us to go now?" Luke asked.

Nillsen looked at Stoneham.

"Sure," Stoneham said. Then he added, "And radio us back as soon as you can."

The two rangers nodded and got up and left the room.

Stoneham turned back to Nillsen. "Can we get somebody out on Oyster Lake tonight—to be waiting in case the man returns?"

Nillsen frowned. "Pretty tough. It's pretty much landlocked. Not just a matter of paddling in with the full moon lighting your way. A lot of portaging."

"How about daylight, then?"

"Sure. A pontoon plane can set down on the water with the first light of day, and let out two or three men." He paused, then added, "That'll work just as well, anyway. The man's not going to be returning to Oyster Lake in the middle of the night."

"Okay. Can you handle the arrangements for me?"

"Sure."

"And tell the men to keep out of sight. We don't want to tip our hand until the man has committed himself."

"Right."

Stoneham turned back to the others seated along the long table. "Anything else? Anything at all?"

The room was silent.

"Okay, that's all," Stoneham said. "And thanks."

As the men got to their feet and filed out of the room, Stoneham stood and turned back to the map. He saw Oyster Lake. He turned his head slightly and saw Snowbank Lake. But the names blurred in his mind as he gritted his teeth and recalled the bedevilment of two strokes of misfortune. There was Sara's failure to deliver the message, which just might have enabled them to get moving in time to intercept the man. Well, no, they probably could not have intercepted him. Lars Nillsen more than likely was correct when he said the man surely left Oyster Lake immediately after learning his whereabouts. Either way, Stoneham resolved to have a talk with Sara. The next message might be more critical. And then there was the bad luck that the discovery of the gear on Snowbank Lake was reported to a ranger who had not attended the morning meeting and did not know of the theory of the stashes. Well, maybe the Snowbank Lake stash did not matter much, except for the information it might reveal. Stoneham sighed. He had to admit that he had gotten more out of the meeting than the bits and pieces he had expected.

"Do you think that's our man—the one on Oyster Lake?" Nillsen was standing at Stoneham's elbow.

The sound of the voice startled Stoneham. "Oh, I thought you'd gone," he said. "Yes, looks like our man. Wouldn't you say so?"

"Yes. He's alone. He doesn't know where he is. He doesn't have any gear. And Oyster Lake is inside the red circle."

"If only we could find the stash he headed for."

Nillsen shrugged. "I don't think that matters much now," he said.

"Oh? Why?"

"I'd bet that the stash he was heading for is no longer a stash. By now, it's a campsite, just like any other campsite, and our man is a camper, just like any other camper."

THE WOODS
Todd and Mike

"Are you awake?"

"Yes."

"Did you hear that?"

"Yes. Shh!"

Todd and Mike lay in silence for a moment in their sleeping bags, unmoving in the darkness, their heads resting on pillows made of canvas bags full of currency. The soft, crunching sound of a foot pressing down on old leaves was unmistakable. A twig broke with a snap that sounded like a rifle shot in the quiet of the night. Then —silence again.

Todd raised himself up on an elbow. He strained his ears for the slightest sound. He tried the impossible—to penetrate the tent wall and the darkness with his eyesight. He heard a shuffling sound. But he could see nothing but darkness.

Mike leaned in toward him. "Do you think it's the hijacker?" he whispered.

"I don't know," Todd whispered back. His fingers fumbled for the button on his digital wristwatch, found it, and pressed it. He squinted down at the glowing figures—almost two o'clock in the morning. It seemed unlikely that anyone would go tramping through the woods in the middle of the night—even a hijacker, enraged and desperate after learning that his loot was gone. It seemed unlikely, too, that anyone wandering the woods in the middle of the night would be able to find a lonely campsite, even if he did come looking. But the man might be frantic enough to make the effort, and lucky enough to succeed.

Todd turned back the cover of his sleeping bag and sat up. He leaned forward and found the flashlight on the tent floor near the door.

"What're you doing?" Mike hissed.

"We've got to check. C'mon, but be quiet."

Mike turned back his sleeping bag cover and sat up, then turned over onto hands and knees, facing the door.

Todd slowly unzipped the tent door. In the silence, the zipper seemed to shriek.

"We'll go out together—and then separate," Todd said. He sensed rather than saw Mike nodding his head in understanding. "If it's the hijacker, we don't want to be in a position where he can come at us both at the same time. Okay?"

"Yeah."

They remained poised on their sleeping bags. The tent door, now unzipped, admitted thin beams of moonlight.

"Get the hatchet."

"Yeah, yeah." Mike made a slight rustling sound as he turned on the sleeping bag and reached to the rear of the tent. "Got it."

From outside the tent, there was nothing but silence.

"Okay, on three."

"Okay."

"One . . . two—three!"

The two boys sprang through the tent door like twin bullets fired from a double-barreled gun. They separated —Todd to the left and Mike to the right of the guyline —and turned. Something—a shadow in the moonlight— jerked back suddenly and then froze in position.

Todd snapped on the flashlight.

He found himself staring into the face of a bear, motionless on all fours, ten feet away. Todd took an involuntary step backward.

He heard Mike, four yards away and a little behind, exhale.

The bear stood without moving, glaring into the light. It didn't seem angry. Rather, it seemed confused, puzzled.

"What do you think?" Mike whispered. "Head for the water?"

A bear—startled, frightened, confused—might be dangerous. Its lumbering stride was deceptive. It could be fleet afoot—faster than a man—and lightning quick with the razor-sharp claws. But a bear was unlikely to pursue its prey into deep water.

"Uh-huh," Todd said, but he hesitated, fearful of making a move that might send the animal into action. Then the bear started retreating away from the glare of the flashlight. "No, wait," Todd told Mike.

The bear backed all the way to the rear of the clearing, then turned and lumbered up the path, beyond the beam of the flashlight and out of sight.

Mike took a deep breath and uttered a small sound—
"Uhhh."

"You bet," Todd said, feeling his heartbeat return to
normal.

"I was almost relieved it was a bear."

"Me, too," Todd said.

DAY THREE

THE WOODS
The Man

He was up before the sun. He came out of the tent buckling his belt. He stood still for a moment in the darkness, staring across the lake toward the east. The first faint rosy hue of the coming day was dusting the dark sky. He listened to the sounds of the early morning in the woods—the stillness broken by the *lap-lap-lap* of the water gently slapping the shore, the *flap-flap-flap* of a bird taking wing, the piercing call of a bird somewhere in the woods behind him. And each time, after the sound, a return to the stillness, the complete stillness of the woods.

The man stretched his arms above his head and then out to the sides, forcing them back as far as they would go. The night on the ground had left a stiffness in his bones. He rubbed his eyes and ran a hand through his hair. He felt the stubble of beard on his chin and resolved to shave. A one-day growth of beard marked a camper as a newcomer in the wilderness, a first-day paddler—the last of all images he wanted to convey to anyone he might encounter. So he would be one of those campers who shaved every day—then who'd be able to say he had not been in the woods for a week?

He squatted down, and then sat, and tied his shoelaces. For several minutes he remained seated, hugging his knees, staring through the darkness at the dim glow rising on the far horizon. This was the day he had planned for —the breakout to freedom and riches.

This was also, he knew, a day of great risk, perhaps the greatest risk of all. The hijacking itself had been risky. But he had been certain all along that the scheme would work if he kept his head. And it had worked. Nobody wanted to take a chance with a stranger who threatened to blow up ninety-six passengers, plus crew. The plunge from the airplane into the darkness also had been risky. But he had leaped from airplanes before, more times than he could count, and this jump was no more dangerous than many of the others. As it turned out, he was luckier in this jump than in some of the past ones. This time, he missed the trees. He had not always been so fortunate. But now came the hours of greatest danger—finding his way out of the woods undetected, slipping through police barricades without arousing suspicion, probably having to answer questions with other campers coming out, arranging to have his gear hauled into town—and all of it while carrying three-quarters of a million dollars past the watchful eyes of police officers. He had kept his head so far. He had measured the odds in capturing the plane and then in parachuting out, and had measured them correctly. He had to keep his head now, as well. But he did not know the odds in today's gamble—the breakout to freedom and wealth.

Getting to his feet, the man stretched his arms again,

took a deep breath, and murmured to himself, "Normal, normal—just keep everything normal." From here on out, he was Byron Matthews, age twenty-eight years, a resident of Tulsa, duly licensed as a driver in the state of Oklahoma. "Here's my driver's license, officer. Is there some problem, officer?" He patted the wallet in the hip pocket of his jeans. He was Bennett Morrison on the airplane's passenger list, but he was Byron Matthews coming out of the woods, and he could prove it. What could be more normal? He would be above suspicion. He was sure of it.

Then he frowned. He knew the disaster awaiting him if the police had succeeded in putting the name Byron Matthews with the black-haired, black-bearded hijacker. But, no, it was impossible. There was no way the police could pin down his identity in such a short time, if ever.

But the frown stayed in place. He remembered the stewardess staring at his eyes—the only undisguised feature he displayed. And he remembered the two boys tramping through the woods toward the lake where the parachute, the clothes, and the money were hidden.

The man shrugged off the troublesome thoughts and walked to the tent and ducked inside. He rummaged through a pack until he found the canoe stove. Stepping out of the tent, he walked to a boulder at the edge of the campsite. Using the huge rock as a windshield, he sat down and began pumping up the pressure in the stove. Satisfied, he opened the valve, struck a match, and ignited a clear blue flame. He waited a moment, watching the flame, and then opened the valve to its limit.

He returned to the tent and found a pot and a canteen in the pack. He walked back to the stove, placed the pot on the stove, and filled it with water.

Funny, he thought, he still was not hungry—no appetite at all. He had had to force himself to eat a tin of dried beef and a couple of pieces of dried fruit the night before. And now, this morning, still not hungry. Nerves, probably. It was just as well. He had no time to spare for preparing and eating breakfast on this day. But a couple of cups of coffee would go down nicely while he shaved, rolled up his sleeping bag, dismantled the tent, and packed the gear in the canoe.

He glanced over his shoulder at the food pack—black against the gray sky—riding high at the end of a rope dangling over a tree limb. He walked to the tree, untied the rope and slowly let out the line, allowing the food pack to descend to the ground. Rolling up the length of rope and dropping it on the ground, he carried the food pack across the clearing and dropped it next to the canoe.

He returned to the tent and stepped inside. On his knees in the darkness he rolled up and tied his sleeping bag. He took it and the small utensil pack out of the tent and placed them on the ground next to the canoe.

The glow of dawn was a little brighter now. There still were no shadows but the sunrise was not far away. The man knew he must waste no time.

The pot on the canoe stove was giving off a faint vapor. The man watched it a moment and then bent over and picked up the utensil pack and the food pack, and carried them across to the canoe stove. From the utensil pack he extracted his thermos mug and a plastic camp cup, and

110

then his razor and the small tube of shaving cream. He laid the items on the ground, then unbuckled the food pack and took out a packet of instant coffee. He opened the packet and poured what he gauged to be a teaspoonful of coffee into the mug, folded the packet, and replaced it in the food pack. He picked up the pot on the canoe stove by its wooden handle and poured water into the mug and the plastic cup. He squatted a moment by the flame, watching the coffee dissolve in the water. Then he took a sip and grimaced at the bitter taste. He put the thermos mug down, sat back, and reached for the plastic cup. Rinsing his face lightly with the warm water, he lathered up, shaved, and wiped his face clean with a paper towel.

When he was finished, the man picked up the mug of coffee again and sat forward, hugging his knees, staring out across the water. The sky was brighter now, and Iron Lake was a dull gray instead of an inky black.

He took a sip of the coffee—again grimacing at the bitter taste—put the cup down, and got to his feet.

The *whack-whack-whack* of the helicopter broke the quiet of the woods, and the chopper, coming across the lake from the man's left, was almost upon him.

He instinctively took a step backward. Then he stopped. There was no reason to hide: he was a camper with tent, canoe, and packs in clear evidence. And there was good reason not to hide. To step behind a tree or duck under a bush would only serve to arouse suspicion. So he stepped forward, turned his face upward, smiled, and waved his right hand as the helicopter, nose down and low, clattered over.

The man watched the helicopter vanish from sight over

a stand of trees. Then he stooped quickly, extinguished the canoe stove, and dumped it in the utensil pack. He poured out the remainder of his coffee and put the thermos mug, along with the pot, his shaving gear, and the plastic cup, in the utensil pack and strapped it shut. He buckled the food pack and carried the two packs across to the canoe. Righting the canoe with his foot, he dropped the packs in.

He moved swiftly to the green pop-up tent and brought it down quickly and easily. He packed the tent into its wrapping and took it to the canoe, dumping it and the sleeping bag in.

He might be just a camper, waving and smiling at a helicopter passing over, but he knew he also was a man alone—a man alone in the woods where a hijacker had parachuted to earth alone. The people in the helicopter, or somebody else, were bound to figure out that the man alone was worth investigating.

He skidded the canoe over the rocky bank and into the water. He tossed in the two paddles and, stepping carefully, got into the stern and seated himself.

The eastern horizon offered a dull orange glow as he paddled away from the bank, heading north.

THE WOODS
Todd and Mike

Todd, the first to awaken, felt a nervousness, and uneasiness. He had not slept well. The bear had not returned, but Todd had not expected it to return. Probably frightened and with no food in evidence making the risk worth the effort, the bear had fled to safety and perhaps a more promising site. No, the encounter with the bear had not contributed to his gnawing feeling of disquiet. But the sounds of the night, instead of being natural and peaceful, had been troubling. Everything seemed to sound like a man walking, a man breathing, a man's clothes rustling. Throughout the night Todd had heard the sounds as he squirmed and turned inside his sleeping bag.

Lifting his head, Todd glanced at Mike in the sleeping bag next to him. Mike, facing away from him, was motionless. The sounds of even breathing told Todd that he was still asleep.

Todd turned back the cover of his sleeping bag and sat up. The tent wall of orange plastic was ablaze with the morning sunlight. Todd glanced at his wristwatch. Five minutes after seven o'clock. "Uh-oh," he groaned. Be-

cause of the night of tossing and rolling, he had slept late
—later than he should have slept. They needed an early
start—earlier than this—for their journey out of the
woods with the money. There always was the danger of
the hijacker coming back, or catching up with them on
their way out.

Todd reached across and shook Mike's shoulder.
"C'mon, roll it out," he said. "It's late. We need to get
moving."

Mike turned slowly to face Todd, stretching his legs
out straight in the sleeping bag as he moved. "Huh? I'm
awake."

"C'mon, for real. Let's go. It's after seven o'clock."

Mike sat up. "Okay."

Todd scrambled out of his sleeping bag and crawled to
the front of the tent. He unzipped the mosquito netting
at the door and stepped outside.

The morning breeze was sending ripples across the
surface of Lake Agnes. The coolness of the breeze felt
good to him.

Unconsciously, he glanced across the campsite and up
at the food bag dangling at the end of a rope over a high
limb. The bear had sniffed out the food, but there was no
way for the animal to get it. Their food was safe.

Todd walked out to the edge of the point protruding
into the water and stood on the large flat rock.

He knew that he and Mike should have headed for the
takeout point with the money right away, the evening
before. There had been time—an easy three hours or so
of daylight left. They could have left their camp behind
them—the tent in place, the food bag tied high—and then

114

returned this morning to resume their journey. By hurrying, and with no gear to slow them down on the portages, they could have made it easily. He sighed. Too late for that now. The important thing now was to get moving.

He turned to give Mike another call and saw him coming out of the tent, rubbing his eyes and blinking in the bright morning sunlight. He walked toward Todd.

"Let's break camp and get started," Todd said. "I don't want to be around here when the man comes back looking for his money."

"Me, either. He's not going to be very happy."

They walked to the tent, ducked inside, and began rolling up their sleeping bags.

"Wait a minute," Mike said. "How about just leaving everything here? We can be back in—what?—by the middle of the afternoon."

Todd shook his head. "I don't think so. If the man catches up with us, or we bump into him somewhere, I don't want us to have just his canvas bags in the canoe. We've got to look as normal as possible. Once we start going back down the Nina-Moose River, it's going to be obvious we're going out—and we wouldn't be doing that without our gear, would we?"

"I guess not."

They rolled up the bags, tied them, and for a moment stared at the canvas bags lying exposed at the end of the tent. Then they put the sleeping bags on top of the canvas bags and backed out of the tent. Better to leave the money bags in the tent, as well hidden as possible, until the last moment.

Outside, Todd walked across and pulled the gear pack

115

out from under the shelter of the overturned canoe and joined Mike back at the tent. They opened the flaps wide and began stowing away items that had spent the night in the tent.

"You know," Mike said, "I've been thinking."

Todd looked at him sharply. He wondered if Mike was going to offer another suggestion that they keep the money.

"I must have been crazy last night. You know, wanting to keep the money." He paused. "I knew better than that."

Todd smiled at him. "Well, we both were thinking about it."

"Were you? Really?"

"Sort of. I couldn't help wondering. You know . . ."

"Wondering what?"

"Wondering if there might be some way that it would be, well, okay to keep it."

Mike grinned at Todd. "That makes me feel better."

Todd put the last item, the flashlight, in the pack, buckled the lid shut, and moved it away from the tent.

They stood up and Todd looked out across the empty lake, glistening in the morning sunlight. "I wonder if he's armed," he said.

"Yeah, I wonder. We could handle him if he's not."

Todd looked at his brawny friend and figured that Mike alone could probably take care of any threat, if the hijacker were unarmed. With the two of them shoulder to shoulder, it certainly would be no contest. But if the hijacker had a gun, that would be another matter.

"He must have had a gun or something to hijack the plane," Mike continued.

"I don't know. You can't just walk onto an airplane with a gun—not with all those metal detectors and things."

"He must have had something."

"They said on the radio that he was threatening to blow up the plane with a bomb."

"Yeah. Maybe that's it. Maybe he's not armed now at all."

"Maybe, but we'd better figure that he's dangerous," Todd said. "Look, you get the food pack and I'll start taking down the tent and we'll be ready to shove off."

"Right."

Todd stepped toward the tent. Out of the corner of his eye he saw Mike at the tree untying the rope that held the food pack. Todd bent over and pulled out one of the stakes that held the guylines taut at the side of the tent.

"Todd," Mike said.

Something in his voice made Todd's heart skip a beat. He straightened and turned. Mike had stopped untying the rope. He was standing still, a hand remaining on the rope.

"Huh? What?" Todd asked. Then his eyes followed Mike's line of sight.

The man, alone, was riding easily on the stern seat in the green canoe, idling in the water a half-dozen yards off the bank. He looked like a man in his late twenties, maybe thirty. He had reddish-blond hair and a smile on his face.

"Good morning," the man called, and waved a hand.

HEADQUARTERS
Agent Stoneham

Ted Stoneham, holding a steaming cup of coffee in his right hand, stood in front of the large map of the BWCA, scanning the names of the lakes and streams. There seemed to be a million of them.

It was seven-thirty and the low rays of the morning sun angled through the window in the opposite wall, casting a bright glare over the endless array of blue shapes signifying the lakes of the BWCA.

Stoneham was alone in the headquarters room, tieless and unshaven, after four restless hours of sleep on the lumpy bed at the Starlite Motel.

From behind him, the voice of Lars Nillsen broke the silence. "What're you looking for?"

Stoneham turned and faced the ranger. "You're up mighty early for a man who was on duty until midnight."

Nillsen shrugged. "I got my sleep."

"We found another weatherbeaten stash—canoe, tent, food pack, the whole works—on Crane Lake. A couple of fishermen reported it this morning."

Nillsen stepped forward and unhesitantly laid a forefinger on the northwest corner of the map—Crane Lake, a large body of water that reached down to the blacktop road at two points.

Stoneham squinted at the map. "Closer to Oyster Lake than Snowbank Lake," he said.

"Uh-huh, but the stash is still there, so it's not the one he headed for."

"You seem so sure he reached the stash he wanted last night."

"I'd bet on it. Say, did Luke and Fred—"

"Yep, they found the Snowbank stash." Anticipating Nillsen's question, he said, "Two paddles, not three." Then he added, "Two paddles at the Crane Lake stash, too."

"So he's alone," Nillsen said slowly.

"I guess so."

"And he didn't want the stash at either Crane Lake or Snowbank Lake."

"Yeah, if the theory is correct."

Nillsen ran a finger across the map—from Crane Lake to Oyster Lake and then the lengthy distance to Snowbank Lake. "He had a stash between Oyster Lake and Snowbank Lake, and that's the one he went for. That's got to be it—a stash between Oyster Lake and Snowbank Lake that was closer than the stash at Crane Lake." He turned to Stoneham. "He had enough daylight to reach it after talking to that couple on Oyster Lake, and he's on his way back to Oyster Lake right now, paddling a canoe and looking just like anybody else. I'd bet on it."

Stoneham sighed. "I hope you're right. A pontoon

plane landed on Oyster Lake at daylight and dropped off three men. So we're ready for him." He paused. "Only thing, I hope we don't scare him away—or catch him too quickly."

"Catch him too quickly?"

"If we grab him too quickly, what have we got? A camper walking through the woods, that's all. Even if his identification shows him to be Byron Matthews, age twenty-eight years, of Tulsa, Oklahoma—what have we got? Just a camper named Byron Matthews—who might, just might, be identified by a stewardess named Gloria Marsh, who last saw him with black hair and a black beard. No, they've got to lay off him until he picks up the money—wherever that might be."

"I see."

"And if they scare him away—if he spots them and then gets away—we've got neither him nor the money. He could wait a month—or a year—before coming back for it."

Nillsen grinned. "I never knew police work was so tough."

"I never imagined that chasing somebody through your woods was so tough."

"Let's get some breakfast."

"I think I'll shave first. I'll meet you at the table in a couple of minutes."

Stoneham, now clean shaven but still tieless, sat at a corner table in Barney's Restaurant with Lars Nillsen. They sipped coffee while waiting for breakfast.

A deputy walked in the front door and headed straight

for the back room before spotting Stoneham and Nillsen. He turned and came over to their table.

"Yes?" Stoneham asked.

The deputy sat down. "A funny report. Maybe nothing."

"What?"

"One of the helicopters spotted a man alone at a campsite . . ."

Stoneham sighed. After the miscues of last night, a wave of trivia was sure to be expected today. Everyone, sensitive to important details being muffed, was now going to relay every splash of a paddle, every snap of a twig. He had seen it happen in investigations before.

"The men in the 'copter didn't think anything was funny at first. They just saw this man alone standing near the edge of the water having a cup of coffee. He waved to them when the 'copter passed over. No way to tell for sure that he was alone. It was the first light of day—barely dawn—and they figured he might have a partner still asleep in the tent."

"Yeah," Stoneham said.

"But they figured it might be worth checking out, so they called in a pontoon plane to land on the lake and take a look."

"And . . ."

"Well, that's the funny part. When the plane landed, everything was gone—the man, his tent, his canoe, everything—cleared out."

"How much time had elapsed?" Stoneham feared he was not going to like the answer.

"Twenty or thirty minutes." The deputy paused and

then added, "The plane was on another lake when the call came and, well, they finished looking around at something there before taking off." He paused again. "I guess they didn't figure the spotting was a really urgent thing."

"I see." Stoneham turned to Nillsen. "Could a man clear out of a campsite in twenty or thirty minutes? And get away? That seems—"

"A man in a hurry can break camp pretty fast. And he can paddle pretty fast, too, if he has to—and then hide; he doesn't have to go far to hide until the plane has left."

"Umm." Stoneham turned back to the deputy. "Where was this?"

"Iron Lake."

"Iron Lake?" Nillsen seemed interested.

"Yeah, Iron Lake."

Stoneham looked at Nillsen. "Does that mean something?"

"It might. Let's look at the map."

The three of them left the table and walked into the back room and across the room to the map on the wall.

"Look at this," Nillsen said, moving a finger across the map. "Here's Oyster Lake. He didn't want to go west from Oyster Lake to Crane Lake for a stash. And there's Iron Lake, between Oyster Lake and Snowbank Lake."

Stoneham squinted at the map. "And closer to Oyster Lake than Crane Lake—a shorter walk to reach the stash."

"Yep."

THE WOODS
Todd and Mike

Todd answered the man's greeting. "Good morning," he said, managing a smile and trying to make his voice sound upbeat.

Mike, still not moving, said nothing.

The man stroked easily with the paddle twice, turning the green canoe gently toward the bank and then back again to a course paralleling the water's edge. With a soft backstroke he brought it to a halt. He laid the paddle across his lap and let the canoe rest in the water, now about ten feet from the bank.

"How's the fishing here?" he asked.

"Caught our dinner last night—three pike," Todd said. Then he added, "Pretty good for starters—our first day in." The words were hardly out when Todd wished he hadn't spoken them. He and Mike would be heading south on Lake Agnes, toward Nina-Moose River and their way out of the woods, not farther in, as would be expected of newly arrived travelers. If the man happened to see them paddling away from their campsite, he was sure to suspect the worst.

The man nodded, keeping the friendly smile in place. "How long have you been in?" Todd asked.

The man's smile seemed to waver slightly. For a flicker of a second he seemed uncertain how to answer. Then he restored his smile. "I had to count 'em up; five days," he said. "I was up on Lac La Croix yesterday. The fishing was great."

"We'll give it a try," Todd said. Again he underscored the fact that he and Mike were just coming in, and indicated they were heading deeper into the woods—not back out. But there seemed nothing else to say.

The man glanced at the tent stake in Todd's hand. "You're breaking camp," he said.

"Just getting packed up," Todd said. And then, fearing that the man might suggest moving into their vacated campsite—and being there to watch them shove off—he added, "Don't know when we'll be moving on, though."

The man's gaze shifted from Todd to the tent—with its open front, the flaps turned back.

Todd felt his hand tremble slightly. The canvas money bags were in the tent—at the head, far inside, with the rolled-up sleeping bags atop them. But they weren't fully covered. Were they visible from the man's perch in the canoe?

"Nice tent," the man said.

For a moment Todd feared the man might want to come ashore and inspect the tent. There would be nothing unnatural about the request. Campers always were interested in other campers' equipment. Todd took a deep breath. "Thanks," he said. "It's not new—a bit weather-beaten, but it works."

124

The man made no move to come ashore. "Was the world still there when you came in yesterday? Anything happening? I've been in here five days, you know, and really out of touch. I like to come in here to get away from everything—and it's good—but we could have World War Three break out and a person in here wouldn't know."

"Yeah, it's true," Todd said. He felt the man's eyes searching his face. The man wanted to know if the boys he had encountered near Oyster Lake were aware of the hijacking. Todd met the man's gaze, smiled, and shook his head. "Nope, not much going on worth talking about, and the world was still there."

"Good," the man said.

After a moment of silence the man said, "I think I'll go down to the end of the lake. Might give the fishing a try, or maybe take a hike in the woods."

"It's a beautiful day for it," Todd said.

"If you're going to be moving on today—didn't you say you might try Lac La Croix?—I might come back and take this campsite. It's a beauty."

Todd glanced at Mike. Mike gave a small shrug. "Don't know yet what we're going to do," Todd said. "We haven't even talked about it."

"It's a nice point. Good breeze, I'll bet."

"Yeah."

"I was camped last night just up there"—he gestured to the north—"coming in from Lac La Croix, you know, and—matter of fact, saw your campfire—and the place was too far back—really buggy when the sun went down, you know."

"Sure," Todd said. He could not help letting his eyes wander to the dead ashes of last night's campfire— blocked from the view from the north by the large boulder the boys had used as a windscreen. Todd looked back at the man and saw that his eyes had followed Todd's to the ashes ringed with stones. Todd felt his heart begin to pound hard in his chest. The man knew he had been caught. "A little flicker of light in the night shows up from a long way off in these woods," Todd said quickly, perhaps too quickly.

"Sure does," the man said. He waved, still smiling, and put the paddle blade in the water. With one long stroke he shot silently away.

Without moving or speaking, the boys watched the man until he and the green canoe, staying close to the bank, disappeared around a point.

Todd inhaled a deep breath, puffed out his cheeks, and exhaled.

"That was him," Mike said. His voice was barely above a whisper. "Same man we saw yesterday."

"Sure was."

"Same shirt—I remember it."

"Yeah."

"He recognized us from yesterday, don't you think? He kept looking at us funny, like he was measuring us up."

"Sure he recognized us. He saw us, same as we saw him." Todd nodded to himself slightly and added, "And he was wondering if we had stumbled on his money bags."

"He's on his way over there now. You heard what he said about taking a hike in the woods."

"Uh-huh, and it's only—what?—about a thirty-minute walk, maybe forty-five minutes, over there. We'd better get moving." He turned toward the tent. "Let's go."

Inside the tent, ready to pull out the sleeping bags and the money bags, Todd stopped. "Wait a minute," he said. "These money bags are too obvious." He began untying his sleeping bag. "C'mon, get that other sleeping bag and let's roll up the money in them." He unfurled his sleeping bag, unzipped the money bag, and began taking out the decks of currency and laying them in rows of four across the sleeping bag.

"Good, yeah." Mike opened the other bag and began spreading the taped stacks of twenty-dollar bills on his bag.

Together, they rolled up their sleeping bags with the rows of money packed inside, then pulled tight and knotted the ropes holding the bundles in their thick cylinder shapes. The bags, each loaded with fifty pounds of twenty-dollar bills, were bulky and heavy. The boys struggled to stuff the bags in plastic trash bags to protect them from any water that might splash into the canoe. Then they shoved the bags out the opening of the tent and crawled out behind them.

"Remember when we timed ourselves setting up camp —a couple of years ago?"

"Yeah," Mike said. "Seven minutes."

"Well, we'd better break camp faster than that this time."

They moved in on the tent, one to a side, pulling the stakes that held the purple fly stretched tight above the tent's roof. They folded the fly and Todd ducked into the tent and got the poles. The tent collapsed. They pulled the stakes and rolled up the tent, with the folded fly bound inside. Then, without bothering to tie up the bundle of tent, they carried it and the sleeping bags to the canoe. Mike finished the job of untying the food pack and lowering it from its lofty dangle.

"Ready?" Todd asked when they met at the canoe.

"Yeah, that's everything."

They righted the canoe and slid it to the water's edge, then loaded their gear into the middle. They scraped the canoe over the last couple of feet into the water, bringing it around parallel to the bank.

Mike stepped into his seat in the bow while Todd held the canoe in a steady position.

Before getting into the canoe, Todd picked up the two empty canvas bags and looked at them. He unbuckled one of the Paul Bunyan packs and stuffed them inside, then rebuckled the pack.

"Okay, let's go," he said, shoving off with his left foot and seating himself in the stern.

THE WOODS

The Man

The man stood looking down at the overturned canoe stashed in a clump of bushes a dozen yards from the water's edge. From the lake, nobody could see it. But from the air, the flicks of silver showing through the scratches in the dull green paint were surely a collection of tiny mirrors reflecting the bright sunlight between the leaves of the bushes.

He bent over the canoe and unbuckled a pack. Opening the flap, he extracted a khaki ground cloth and spread it out over the forward half of the canoe. He picked up rocks and placed them at the corners of the ground cloth. Then he pulled out another ground cloth and covered the after half of the canoe, again weighting down the corners with rocks.

He straightened up and surveyed the scene for a moment, then gave a barely perceptible nod of approval. He glanced back out over the lake. Nobody there. He considered waiting a moment to see if the boys pulled out—and, if so, which way they were heading. But no, he did not have the time to spare. Besides, the boys seemed in no hurry. They had not yet even begun preparing breakfast.

He walked away from the lake, headed west—the direction of Oyster Lake. At the top of the first rise in the ground he stopped and took the folded map out of his shirt pocket. He opened the map and stood, motionless, studying the crazy-quilt pattern of lakes and streams.

The route was simple: due west to a tiny stream, maybe twenty or so minutes away; then north with the stream for a few yards; then west with the stream to Oyster Lake.

The man took a deep breath, folded the map, and replaced it in his shirt pocket; then he walked through the woods, the morning sun to his back.

He had gone only a few steps, shoving his way through the trackless woods, when he heard the sound of a helicopter. He flattened himself against a tree, partly hidden from above by the leaves, and scanned the sky. He saw nothing. The *whack-whack-whack* of the whirling blades began to weaken and fade. The helicopter was going away, off to the west. Finally the sound died out completely. The man stepped out from under the tree. He made a mental note to watch for possible hiding places— a tree with thick foliage, a large shrub—as he moved along, and to hurry across the open places. After all, the helicopter had faded out of earshot to the west—the direction he was heading.

When he came upon the tiny unnamed stream, he remembered jumping from one rock to another in crossing the water yesterday. Was it only yesterday? It seemed now to be a week—maybe a month—ago. This time, though, was as different as day and night from yesterday's journey. Now he was heading for the money, not leaving it behind.

130

As he moved northward along the stream, occasionally stepping into the shallow water at the edge with a splash, he wondered again about the boys. No doubt they were the same two he had met in the woods on his way from Oyster Lake. They had pitched their camp and taken advantage of the last hours of daylight to explore in the direction of Oyster Lake. Had they spotted him? Sure, same as he had seen them. Had they recognized him this morning? Maybe so, maybe not. To him, they had been little more than shadowy forms in the woods yesterday. Probably he had been only the same to them. But still the question put a frown on the man's face. If they did recognize him, they had him caught in the lie about spending the day before fishing in Lac La Croix to the north. He should have thought through his story more carefully. He should have thought more carefully, too, before dropping the remark about seeing their campfire the night before. The taller one, the boy who did all the talking, spotted it for a lie. His glance at the fireplace next to the boulder was a dead giveaway. But then the boy let him off the hook, saying something about a fire being visible for miles in the woods. The man wondered why the boy said it. There was something strange about it all, and he continued to frown as he picked his way along the stream.

How far had the boys gone toward Oyster Lake? There was daylight enough for them to go all the way. If they reached the lake, did they stumble across the blue dress suit, the parachute—and the canvas bags filled with money—in the clump of bushes? Maybe.

But no, no, it was impossible. It simply was incredible that in all of these acres—thousands of square miles of woods—two campers taking an afternoon hike would happen to come together with the stash at the right time and the right place to make the discovery. No, the odds of it happening could only be measured in terms of light-years.

But what if they did find the money? They certainly would not leave it there under the bushes. No, they would take it—where?—back to their camp. And then what? Would they simply resume their canoe camping trip, sleeping through the night, fixing themselves a leisurely breakfast, planning some fishing—all with three-quarters of a million dollars packed in their gear? No, no, of course not. They would have headed out—to turn in the money, or to get away with it. No, they had not found the money.

The stream made a ninety-degree turn to the left and the man turned with it, again heading due west.

Now, about a half-mile to go.

Again, the *whack-whack-whack* of a helicopter sent the man scurrying for cover. He leaped instinctively toward a hiding place—a spruce tree with low branches—and ducked under just as the aircraft came over the treetops to the south of him. Peering between the branches at the sky, he wondered if hiding were the wisest move. He could explain walking through the woods—just a camper on a hike—with a banked canoe and the gear to prove it. But if spotted racing for cover, he could say only—what? Nothing. He considered striding out from under the cover of the spruce in full view of the helicopter and the portion of a face pointed toward the ground. But, no.

Undoubtedly the chopper would land. There would be questions. Better to avoid questions. Better to avoid being seen. He resolved to move more carefully, make his way through the thicker growth, keep himself hidden as much as possible.

The helicopter roared over him and disappeared to the north. The man moved out from under the cover of the tree and back to the bank of the stream, where he resumed picking his way along among the rocks.

When Oyster Lake came into view he halted, then moved back and to the side into a cover of trees and sat down. He was hidden if the helicopter returned. He pulled the map out of his shirt pocket and unfolded it. He stared at it, trying to orient himself. He was a bit south of the clearing where the money was stashed. He turned to his right—to the north—and looked up the rise. That was where the money was waiting.

A helicopter roared over. The man sat still under the trees, hugging his knees, his face down. Why were all of these 'copters buzzing around like flies? One was to be expected every now and again, because the police were surely crisscrossing the area. But why so much activity around Oyster Lake? It did not make sense.

Unless . . .

He thought of the boys again. If they had found the money and reported their discovery—then the explanation was simple: the police knew their man would be returning to Oyster Lake sooner or later to pick up the ransom, and they needed only to await his arrival.

But even if the boys had found the money, how could

they have reported their discovery? They were camped on Lake Agnes, talking about going fishing. It did not make sense. Not at all.

The helicopter was moving away. The man was gripped by an almost overwhelming desire to run up the rise to the clearing, to confirm that the money was there —safe, undiscovered, undisturbed. But he sat still until the sound of the 'copter, now in the distance, faded away to complete silence.

He stepped out from under the tree cover slowly and glanced around—down toward the bank of Oyster Lake, again up the rise to the north, and back into the woods he had come from. The sense of excitement was gone from him. He no longer had the pleasurable feeling that everything was going well. He felt a strong need for caution—extreme caution. He did not know why, but he suddenly felt that things were going bad on him. After all the planning, all the risks, all the good luck—things were turning from good to bad. He could sense the shift in fortune.

The woods were still. Nothing moved. There was no sound. Oyster Lake was placid, as smooth and flat as a sheet of glass.

He saw the glint—sunlight bouncing off metal—out of the corner of his eye, to his left. It was a flicker, tiny and brief. He turned his face toward it, and he saw, for just a fraction of a second, the unmistakable form of a man. The form vanished in the thick woods back from the lake shore.

The man jerked himself back toward the cover of trees so quickly that he stumbled and almost fell. The scrambling noise of his feet scraping the ground seemed to echo like thunder in the silent woods. He froze in his tracks. Then he edged himself backward toward the cover of trees, scanning the woods where the form had flashed into view and then disappeared. He saw nothing.

What now?

The man sat down. He had a clear line of sight to the woods where he had seen the figure. He waited and watched. Nothing. Nothing at all. Perhaps it was a camper—a chance encounter. And perhaps the camper had simply moved on, into the woods, away from Oyster Lake.

The man got to his feet. He glanced to his right, up the rise, toward the clearing where the money awaited him.

He moved up the rise and to his right, staying back in the woods, walking slowly, stopping every few steps to listen to the silence of the woods.

He stopped short of the clearing and looked around— at the woods surrounding the clearing, at the sky where a helicopter might suddenly appear, and at the woods behind him where someone might be coming up on him at this very moment. All was still, quiet, empty.

He edged his way around the clearing.

He saw the clump of blueberry bushes and headed toward it. He stopped and looked around again. Nothing. He hurried toward the bushes. Reaching them, he bent low, pushed aside the loose dirt and leaves, and pulled out the bundle—the blue suit and parachute. Dropping it on the ground, he bent back into the bushes and looked around, and he found—nothing.

He stared at the ground. He got down on his hands and

knees and crawled under the bushes, scratching the ground with his fingers. When he still found nothing, he backed out and stood up. Then he bent, picked up the bundle of the suit and the parachute and shook it, as if the canvas bags might fall out of the folds.

Nothing.

He felt his face flush with sudden warmth. His shoulders sagged. His breath was coming hard.

He looked to his left, toward Lake Agnes, a mile or so through the woods.

Then, leaving behind the pile of fabric, he jogged back into the woods, heading for the small unnamed stream that would lead him back to the shores of Lake Agnes.

THE WOODS
Todd and Mike

"Let's pull over a minute," Todd said.

"Huh?"

"Just for a minute. I want to look at this map."

They had paddled their way across Lake Agnes and moved through the mouth of the Nina-Moose River. The lazy, drifting current of the stream was barely discernible. Beyond the mouth of the river, the Nina-Moose narrowed quickly to a slender corridor of water. Trees and bushes pressed in closely from both sides.

Todd held his paddle blade in the water at the stern, steering them toward the bank, while Mike paddled.

At the bank, Mike turned and looked at Todd. "What is it?"

Todd had the map out of his pocket and was unfolding it. "Something just occurred to me." He frowned at the map. "Yeah," he said.

"What?"

"Look at this."

Mike stepped out onto the bank and walked back along the canoe. As he walked, he glanced across the mouth of the Nina-Moose River and toward the horizon on Lake Agnes. It was empty. He bent over Todd's shoulder and looked at the map.

"We're here," Todd said, pointing to the spot on the map where the Nina-Moose River emptied into Lake Agnes. "And the man is here"—he shifted his finger to Oyster Lake—"just discovering that his money is missing."

"Uh-huh."

"He's going to come after us. He saw us heading for the area yesterday after he had left the money there. He's got to figure that we found the money and that we've got it. There's no other way."

"Sure, but I don't—"

"But he's not going to go back to our campsite on Lake Agnes."

"What do you mean?"

"Look, he's going to figure that we were going to do exactly what we're doing—getting out of the woods as quickly as we can. He knows we saw him over there yesterday. He knows we saw him this morning. He even said he might take a hike, so he knows that we knew he was headed for the money—heading for discovering that it was gone. So he's going to figure that we're not likely to sit around a campsite and wait for him to come back. He's going to know that we're heading out—but fast—and he's going to know our route."

"Okay, but so what?"

"So instead of wasting almost an hour walking back to our campsite and then starting to paddle after us—especially with us having a head start of an hour or so—he's going to go straight south—just a couple of miles through the woods—and hit the Nina-Moose River about there—maybe ahead of us, so he can be there waiting."

Mike stared down at the map, watching Todd's moving finger. "Oooh," he said. "I see."

Todd lifted his head and stared ahead at the trees, as if they might offer advice.

"What do you think we ought to do?" Mike asked.

"I don't know. Let me think a minute."

"There are two of us and just one of him."

Todd glanced at Mike. "Unless he's armed," he said.

"He wouldn't want to fire a gun," Mike said. "In these woods, a shot would be heard all the way into Ely."

"Yeah, you're right."

"We've got our knives."

Todd shook his head. "Wait a minute. Let me think."

The woods were quiet and still, a mix of deep green and brown under a light blue sky with soft wisps of cloud—an unlikely setting for an act of violence by a desperate man.

"First, we've got to try to beat him to the point where he is going to intersect the Nina-Moose. If we can do that, we'll be home free. He'll stop to wait for us, and maybe even go up and down the river looking for some trace of us, and all the while we'll be pulling farther away from him."

"And if we don't beat him?"

"If we don't . . ." Todd let the sentence trail off.

"I can't imagine him trying to jump us in the water,"

Mike said. "What's he going to do, wade out after us?"

"Yeah, I think you're right."

"But the portages . . ."

"Yeah, that's where we might run into trouble."

They both bent over the map again and studied the portages ahead of them—one of sixty-five rods and another of seventy rods on the Nina-Moose River, and then after passing through Nina-Moose Lake, three more on the Moose River—nine rods, twenty rods, and a big one of one-hundred seventy-seven rods.

"That last one—the big one—doesn't matter," Todd said. "That's the one leading to the takeout point. We can leave the canoe and run for it. There are bound to be police—"

Todd stopped and he and Mike looked at each other. Then Mike said what was in both their minds: "What if the police don't even know that he and the money are in this area? When he bailed out, he might have landed anywhere. What if they're looking in other places, and we don't find anything but a couple of campers at the takeout point?"

Todd shook his head. "Nah, nah," he said. "The plane and the helicopter we saw—they're sure signs that the police are hunting for him around here."

"I hope so."

"Yeah."

"I wish one of those choppers would come over now, real low," Mike said.

"Uh-huh."

"Look, why don't we leave the canoe now—just take off through the woods on a straight line for the road. It can't be more than a few miles, and we've got a head start. Even if he finds the canoe, he won't know which way we went. He won't be able to catch us."

Todd wrinkled his brow. Mike had a good point. They could repack the money in the canvas bags and strike out to the south. He glanced down at the map—six or seven miles from here to the road. Through trackless woods, that probably meant three or four hours of walking, carrying the heavy money bags.

"No," Todd said finally. "If he found our canoe, it wouldn't take a genius to figure out which way we had gone. I think we're better off being in the canoe on the water, and we'll just have to be careful on the portage paths."

"I guess so."

"And we'd have a better chance of maybe running into some policemen or rangers—or maybe even just campers —if we stick to the streams and the paths. Just having the company of some other campers would help."

"You can say that again," Mike said. "Okay, let's make miles."

"Right."

In less than an hour they dragged the canoe ashore at the start of the first portage.

"From here on, our path might cross with his any-where," Todd said.

Mike nodded, and they both bent over to pull out the gear and get themselves organized for the portage—sixty-five rods along a narrow, hard-packed pathway through the woods.

Their gear, tossed into the canoe so hastily at the Lake

Agnes campsite, was a mess, and they needed ten minutes to pack properly for the portage—the food pack, one sleeping bag, and the tent in one huge Paul Bunyan pack, and the utensil pack and the second sleeping bag in the other pack.

"Ready?"

"Ready."

Their packs strapped to their backs, they bent over the canoe, rolled it up over their heads, and began packing toward the next navigable stretch of the Nina-Moose River.

THE WOODS
The Man

The man, holding his compass in his left hand, thrashed through the woods at a half-run pace, keeping the morning sun to his left, heading due south. He weaved through the clumps of trees, carefully correcting his course as he went. He shoved his way through bushes, ignoring the scratches inflicted on his hands and arms by the branches.

At each rise in the land he stopped, breathing heavily, and consulted his compass, confirming the direction the morning sun was giving him as he ran. And each time, he looked also at his wristwatch and frowned: the minutes seemed to be flying by. And he looked back, squinting at the last rise in the land, to see if anyone was on his trail, closing in, catching up with him.

He foolishly had left the bundle of the parachute and the blue suit where he had dropped it, in clear view of a helicopter or a pontoon plane passing over. In the panic that struck with the realization that the money was gone, he had had only one thought: catch the boys. He was into the woods, more than a couple of hundred yards away, before he remembered the splash of white silk on the ground inviting discovery. He had whirled around so quickly he almost fell, starting the dash back to gather up the fabric and hide it. But then had come the sound— *whack, whack, whack*—and a helicopter, nose down, had fluttered along the bank of Oyster Lake, gone up the rise, and stopped in the air above the parachute and the suit. The man had slammed on the brakes, whirled again, and resumed his dash away from the lake. This time, though, he changed his route. He had no need to return to Lake Agnes. The boys would not be there. They would be on their way out. His route was due south, to cut them off. Part of his brain, at least, was functioning.

Pushing through the woods, taking his breath now in huge gulps, the man tried to sort out his thoughts. His mind was cluttered with regretful second-guessing.

The discovery of the parachute and the blue suit was sure to bring every policeman in the BWCA to the area around Oyster Lake. They were going to be tightening the ring and coming after him. He had to recover his money and escape before the ring was locked tight.

He knew there were rangers who could track a trail in the woods as easily as most travelers followed the pavement of an interstate highway. His thrashing progress through the woods was leaving all the telltale signs— trampled leaves, crushed and broken bushes—that a veteran ranger needed. The man knew he might as well be posting signs along the way. But it was going to take time for the helicopter pilot to land and identify his discovery, time to radio back the word of the find, time to bring in people for the hunt, and time for the trackers to locate the

144

start of the trail. And all this time added up. He would, at least, have a head start.

Unless . . .

The man's mind went back to the figure that flashed into view and then disappeared in the woods at Oyster Lake. The form might have been that of a ranger, and he might not have been alone. The helicopter might not have had to radio for help to launch the pursuit. The help might be already there, on the ground. The trackers might already be giving chase.

The thought spurred him to faster—ever faster—movement through the woods.

Everything now seemed to be a mistake, and each one swirled around in the man's mind. He never should have left the money behind. It had all seemed so sure, so logical, so right—hide the money until he was outfitted with canoe, tent, all the gear of an ordinary camper. Don't carry the money until all the appearances of a normal canoe camper were in place. But he should have taken the money with him to the stash. He should have known he could avoid close encounters with other campers, as in fact he had done. He would be on his way out—or already be out—by this time, a free man, and rich, instead of frantically trying to catch two boys in front of him and outrun the police who surely were behind him.

He should have . . . should have . . . should have.

"Stop it," he said aloud.

He tried to wipe from his mind the errors he had made and to concentrate instead on what to do now. What, indeed?

He was caught in a tightening vise. He had to reach the boys ahead of him before the police caught up with him from behind. He was no longer shielded in innocence by the fact of not having the money in his possession. He was running away from the parachute on the ground, and he had no answer to give the police if they caught up with him and asked him why.

The distant chopping sound of a helicopter in flight sent the man stumbling toward a pair of trees with low-hanging branches. He dropped to the ground and scrambled around one of the tree trunks, peering upward and to the south, in the direction of the approaching *whack-whack-whack* sound.

The helicopter came in low over the trees, to his right, and roared overhead and away to the north.

The man turned and sat motionless for a moment, his back against the tree trunk. He had escaped detection. He was sure of it. But the chopper might double back. So he decided to remain where he was. Besides, a couple seconds of rest, leaning back against the tree, felt good. He still was breathing heavily.

After a few moments, the man got to his feet. He glanced at the compass, still held in his left hand, and looked up, following the line to the south. Then he looked at his wristwatch and frowned. How could so much time have passed? He jogged away from the protective cover of the trees.

He thought once again of what might have been, if only . . .

"Stop it," he ordered himself again.

146

He had to have a plan for dealing with the boys once he caught up with them—and he was going to catch them. He was sure of it. He *had* to. But where would it be—on a lake, a stream, a portage path? What if he caught up with them on a lake? Then there'd be nothing to do but watch and follow. He could hardly swim out to them and ask for his money. And what if he caught them on a stream? If narrow enough and shallow, a stream might not be a bad place to make his move. The man nodded unconsciously at the thought as he picked his way through a stand of small spruce trees. What if he caught up with them on a portage path? That would be the best of all. Lying in wait for them, as they struggled under the weight of their canoe and gear, he would have a physical advantage as well as the element of surprise to make his move.

His move? What move?

The man toyed with the idea of trying to strike a bargain with them: "Look, you give me one bag and you keep the other bag, and I'll go my way and you go yours, and we'll all be happy. Okay?" The boys surely wanted money. Everyone did. And this way, everyone involved would get some money—lots of money. Maybe the boys would buy the deal. He hoped so, because that would be the best way—quick, quiet, clean. Even though he hated the prospect of giving up some of the money, getting away with half of it was better than getting away with none—and maybe being caught and jailed to boot.

Then the man shook his head. The boys would not buy the deal. Why should they? If they intended to turn the money in to the police, that was that. There would be no deal to talk about. And if they intended to keep the money for themselves, why would they smilingly agree to give half of it away? No, they would fight—or run.

So what was his move?

Before the man could begin to try to answer the question, he halted suddenly. He turned slightly to his right. Then he stood still. There had been a sound, a sound of movement, off to the right, away from his own rustling noises. Now there was only silence. Then the man heard the sound again. He turned his head a bit more to the right and held his breath.

Twenty yards away the bushes quivered crazily and two bear cubs darted out and vanished behind another clump of shrubs.

The man exhaled a long breath. He felt relief, but only for a moment. Where was the mother bear? The bears of the BWCA usually presented no serious danger to anyone who exercised normal caution. But a mother bear separated from her cubs by the threatening figure of a man became a raging killer. The man felt his heart pounding at a rapid pace. He looked around and listened, but saw and heard nothing, not even the movement of the cubs.

Then, off to his right, where the cubs had vanished behind a group of bushes, he saw a flash of brownish-black fur. It was the rambling form of the mother bear seeking her cubs.

His heart slowed its pounding. He realized the palms of his hands were wet with perspiration and wiped them absently on his jeans. He looked at the compass, then the wristwatch, and moved away.

Again, he wondered, what was his best move when he caught up with the boys?

HEADQUARTERS
Agent Stoneham

The deputy, a rawboned man in his twenties, wearing khaki trousers, a faded red sports shirt, and a Minnesota Twins baseball cap perched on the back of his head, burst through the door. "They've found his stuff," he said.

Stoneham looked up sharply. "His stuff? The money?"

"Well, no, not the money."

"Then what?"

The deputy walked across to the table. He was carrying a small map detailing a section of the BWCA. He sat down next co Stoneham and across from Lars Nillsen. He spread out the map. "Up on Oyster Lake," he said. "The parachute, and a blue suit of clothes."

"But no money."

"No. They've looked everywhere. The money's not there."

"And the man—any trace of him?"

The deputy nodded. "Sort of. Jacob thinks he spotted him but then lost him in the woods."

"Jacob?"

"He's one of the chopper pilots," Nillsen said.

Stoneham nodded and turned back to the deputy. "Take it from the beginning. Just tell me what's happened, in the order in which the things occurred."

The young deputy frowned in thought for a moment.

"This was a radio report received in the sheriff's office?"

"Yes."

"Just tell me the information like you were telling a story, from beginning to end."

"Okay. Well, Jacob was moving back and forth over the area around Oyster Lake, you know, after the man was spotted there all alone without any gear yesterday."

Stoneham nodded gently, trying to hide his impatience. He knew the young deputy had no experience taking and giving reports. He had just happened to be in the sheriff's office when the report came in, and it had fallen his lot to relay the information to the FBI agent from Minneapolis. Stoneham knew, too, that the young deputy in this rural county possibly was nervous delivering a report to the FBI agent from Minneapolis. But even while knowing these things, Stoneham still wished mightily that the deputy would get on with the business of delivering the hard facts.

"Jacob was making a pass over the eastern bank when he thought he saw a man sitting on the ground under a spruce tree. When he swerved to go back for another look —he took a big arc, you know, because he was supposed to be kind of casual and not scare the man away—he saw this bundle on the ground next to a clump of bushes. He kept going in his arc, but when he got back he couldn't find the man again." He paused. "The man had either run away or he had hidden himself better."

"Go on."

"Well, Jacob went back and put down in a clearing and ran over to the bundle. It was the parachute and the blue suit, all bunched up into a kind of loose bundle."

"But no money?"

"No." The young deputy's downcast expression seemed to say that he felt personally responsible for the failure to find the money. "The others came over when they saw the chopper land, and they all hunted everywhere for the money."

"I see," Stoneham said with a sigh.

"They looked everywhere for the money," the deputy repeated.

"Okay," Stoneham said, frowning. He looked at Nillsen. "He's out there somewhere in the woods with two canvas bags full of money slung over his shoulders."

"I'd say it looks that way."

"On foot," Stoneham said, more to himself than the others.

"Oh, that reminds me." The deputy glanced from Stoneham to Nillsen. "Just before that, Jacob spotted what he thinks is a canoe covered by some ground cloth —a kind of funny way to leave a canoe, unless something funny is going on."

Stoneham glanced at Nillsen. "Anything?"

"Maybe. A camper worried about it raining on his gear usually just turns over the canoe to protect the gear beneath it. But, now, if you didn't want your canoe spotted from the air . . ."

"Where was this?" Stoneham asked.

"Lake Agnes—the west bank."

Nillsen nodded. "He must have left the canoe there and walked over to Oyster Lake, figuring to carry the money back to the canoe, stow it deep inside his gear somewhere, and—"

"Yes, yes," Stoneham said quickly. "And then paddle his way to some takeout point and be gone."

Nillsen nodded.

"Let's get over to the sheriff's office and have them radio a pontoon plane to set down on the—what was it? —west bank of Lake Agnes."

Out on the street, heading across to the sheriff's office, Nillsen said, "Look, you're the FBI agent, and I'm not arguing with putting some men with that canoe, but—"

"But what?"

"Well, I wouldn't count on our man returning to that canoe now."

"Oh?"

They stepped up the curb, crossed the sidewalk to the door of the sheriff's office, and walked in.

"We can't chance it," Stoneham said. "We've got to cover everything we can."

"No argument," Nillsen said, shrugging his shoulders.

Stoneham turned to the deputy manning the radio. "Can you raise a pontoon plane to go to Lake Agnes and locate a canoe under a groundcloth on the west bank— and watch out for a man approaching it? He might be our hijacker."

"Sure," the deputy said, throwing a switch and leaning into the microphone.

153

Stoneham turned back to Nillsen. "You don't think he'll return to the canoe?"

"Well, I know I wouldn't," Nillsen said. "Look, he probably knows he's been spotted. He also probably knows that we've found the parachute and the suit of clothes. He may even have been watching from the woods when Jacob set down. So he knows he's been pinpointed. And there he is, carrying the money around. What would you do?"

"Run as fast and as far as I could."

"Sure, but not to where you're likely to be spotted."

Stoneham nodded. "I see. We can scoop up everyone on the lakes and streams and paths with no trouble. But finding someone in the woods is another matter."

"Exactly."

"A needle in a haystack," Stoneham muttered. "Worse yet, a needle that's moving around in the haystack."

"He'll leave a trail."

"But there's no telling which way he's run."

"He's trying to get out, not go deeper inside, now that he knows we've got him spotted. His only hope now is to break out, isn't it?"

Stoneham stared at a map of the BWCA under a cracked glass on a desktop. He wasn't looking for anything in particular, but the words "Oyster Lake" jumped out at him. He looked at the small blue spot, with the black line of Echo Trail running below it. "He'd head straight south, you think?"

"I'd bet on it."

"Ummm. Lots of territory there."

"Phil Schuyler is out there with the rest of them," the young deputy offered.

Stoneham glanced at the deputy. "Phil Schuyler?" he asked, missing the significance of the name.

"Phil Schuyler," Nillsen said with a grin. "Well, it's been said that he once tracked a field mouse four miles through the woods."

The young deputy laughed. "If anybody could do it, Phil could."

Stoneham nodded and gave Nillsen a small smile. "Okay," he said with a shrug, "Phil Schuyler, do your stuff."

A couple of minutes later the deputy at the radio called out that a pontoon plane was over Lake Agnes.

"Good," Stoneham said.

Then the radio crackled with the word that Phil Schuyler had found not one but three trails leading away from the east bank of Oyster Lake—all of them recent.

Stoneham and Nillsen leaned forward as the voice described the trails. Two of them led due east toward Lake Agnes. One of them led almost due south, and seemed the freshest of the three.

"Tell them," Stoneham said, "to take the one going south."

THE WOODS
Todd and Mike

At the end of the portage, Todd and Mike lowered the canoe into the water. Standing up, with the huge packs still on their backs, they both glanced back down the portage path behind them. It was empty. They looked up the river ahead of them, and at the woods spread out on both sides. All was quiet, still.

"Well, that's one," Todd said softly.

"Do you think we're past him—past the point where he might cross our path?"

Todd pulled the map out of his shirt pocket, unfolded it, and stared down at it. "Maybe," he said. "Anyway, the chances get better with every yard we move."

"Then let's get going."

"Right."

They shucked the packs and dumped them into the center of the canoe. Todd bent over and held the stern steady while Mike stepped into the bow and took his seat. Then Todd shoved the canoe forward slightly, stepped easily into the stern, and sat down.

"Okay," Todd said.

Both paddles bit deeply into the water, and the red canoe shot forward in the lethargic stream.

They had barely hit their stride—the smooth meshing of the bow paddler's powerful strokes and the stern paddler's guiding strokes—when the second portage loomed in front of them. They both leaped out into water up to their calves and dragged the canoe onto the bank.

Pulling on a pack, Todd said, "You know, there's something funny."

"Funny? What?"

"There's nobody coming in."

"Yeah, you're right."

"Anybody getting an early start on a trip this morning ought to be, well, right around here by now, wouldn't you think?"

"Uh-huh," Mike said slowly. He hoisted the pack onto his back.

Todd glanced at his wristwatch. "It's almost nine o'clock," he said. "Maybe it's still a little early." His voice carried a tone of uncertainty, as if he were trying to convince himself but not quite succeeding.

Mike looked around. "Yeah, maybe," he said.

"Let's get going."

They bent and grabbed the struts of the canoe, rolled it up their bodies and over their heads, and began tramping the seventy rods of hard-packed trail to the next stretch of navigable water on the Nina-Moose River.

The rhythmic *thump-thump-thump* of their footsteps seemed to echo in the stillness of the woods.

Two-thirds of the way along the straight path, a sound

of heavy movement in the underbrush to their left brought them to a halt. They peered in the direction of the noise.

"See anything?" Todd asked, his voice hardly above a whisper.

"No."

"Probably a deer."

"Or a hijacker," Mike said.

"Funny, funny. Let's go."

At the end of the path, with the canoe resting in the shallow water at the bank, they again glanced back down the path, then up the river ahead, and into the thick woods on both sides of the water. They saw nothing, heard nothing.

Todd pulled out the map and gave it a quick look. "This stretch of river will get us into Nina-Moose Lake." He dumped his pack into the canoe. Mike's pack followed. "It'll feel good to get out onto a lake for a while and away from these woods coming in so close."

"I thought my heart was coming up into my throat when we heard that noise back there."

"Me, too."

Mike stepped to the bow of the canoe. "Ready?"

"Ready." Todd held the canoe while Mike stepped in, then shoved off and stepped into the stern. "Okay, set," he said, and they dug their paddles into the water.

"How far?" Mike asked, speaking over his shoulder.

"Mile . . . mile and a half, maybe."

"Still nobody coming in," Mike said, his voice barely audible, as if he were speaking to himself.

Todd did not answer.

THE WOODS
The Man

Thrashing his way through the dense underbrush, the man came upon the small stream so suddenly that he almost stepped into the water.

He halted his forward plunge abruptly and looked down at the water. The stream was a narrow trickle of water—too narrow and shallow to be the Nina-Moose River. He pulled the map out of his shirt pocket and unfolded it. He squinted at the map. This had to be the small unnamed stream on the map crossing between Oyster Lake and Nina-Moose Lake, flowing out of Ramshead Lake. The man focused on Oyster Lake and moved his gaze due south to the point where it intersected with the creek. The Nina-Moose River was there. He must surely be only a few yards from the point where the creek joined the Nina-Moose River, a mile or so below Lake Agnes.

He looked at his wristwatch—nine o'clock, almost on the dot.

The boys in the red canoe, unless they were slower than he thought, were a mile or two ahead of him on the Nina-Moose River, approaching Nine-Moose Lake. And unless they were dumber than he thought, they were paddling hard. They were pulling away from him with every second that he stood still.

The man wasted no more time. Pocketing the map, he crossed the stream, wading in ankle-deep water, stepping on rocks when he could, and picked up a portage path on the other side. He broke into a run.

Barely minutes later the stream ended in a narrow river —the Nina-Moose, for sure.

Without stopping to consult his map again, the man turned right and ran along the bank. He stuffed the compass in his pocket. No need to check direction now. He was on the trail he needed to follow.

For the most part the bank was clear—grass, with a few bushes—and he pressed himself to keep jogging in order to take fullest advantage of the running room. Plenty of time to rest when dense woods forced him to slow his pace.

Twice he came upon narrow pathways running parallel to the river. Perhaps the river had been lower a hundred years ago or more, or maybe rockier, and these were old portage paths used by the trappers.

Twice he heard the *whack-whack-whack* of a helicopter and once the whirring sound of a small airplane's engine, and he dived into the cover of bushes, where he lay motionless, hugging his knees, until the noise faded away. Then he resumed running.

As he ran, the question returned to his mind: What was the best move when he caught up with the boys? He had to have a plan.

"Think, think, think," he told himself as he swung

around a tree growing crookedly at the river's edge.

Words raced through his mind at the rat-a-tat pace of machine-gun bullets: violence, the threat of physical injury, danger of death. Those were the kinds of words that somehow were going to provide the answer he needed. Those were the kinds of things that would make the boys turn over the money. But how to pull it off? He was not armed. With his plan, he hadn't needed a gun to hijack the airliner. The phoney bomb had done the job. And later, in the woods, a gun would only have cast suspicion on him if it was discovered. He had his hunting knife. Maybe that would do it. Or a stick of wood wielded as a club? Maybe just bare hands—a knotted fist, strangling fingers?

The man shuddered visibly and shook his head as he ran. He hated violence. The thought of inflicting injury, maybe even death, on another human being was repugnant to him, almost to the point of physical sickness. As a paratrooper, he had hated and feared the weapons he had to handle. Even in the plane during the hijacking, he knew he would have allowed himself to be taken prisoner before he would have hurt anyone.

But now—what else but violence?

Ah, the *threat* of violence—if he could pull it off.

The undergrowth was thickening along the riverbank, and the trees were more numerous. The man had to slow his pace in order to shove his way through bushes and to weave his way through the patch of saplings.

At every bend, he slowed and gazed up the river ahead. It was important that he spot the boys before they saw him.

161

Heading away from him, they would have their backs to him when he caught up to them. That was a help, and an advantage he did not want to lose. But it would be lost if he came upon them noisily and they turned. Probably now he was still many minutes, perhaps even as much as an hour, behind them. But it was never too early to be careful.

The man tried to picture himself menacing two sturdy teenaged boys, presenting sufficient threat to make them turn over money they either intended to keep for themselves or to deliver to the police.

The threat had to be immediately obvious and seriously dangerous—but also clearly escapable. The boys had to be able to see instantly that there was a way of avoiding the danger and getting out unharmed if they complied with his demands. Otherwise, desperation would take over, and that would be a disaster. The man knew he could not handle two teenaged boys who had passed over the brink into desperation, believing they were fighting for their very lives. No, he had to threaten them, but in such a way that they knew the better course was to hand over the money; that there was no need to fight for their lives.

The man resumed jogging along a stretch of clear riverbank.

So what was the best move to make? His mind offered no suggestions. He saw clearly what he needed to accomplish. But how?

"Put yourself in their shoes," he murmured half aloud. "Sure, that's it."

The man tried to picture himself as a teenager, carrying

162

a fortune in stolen cash, paddling a canoe toward the edge of the wilderness, being pursued by a desperate and possibly dangerous man who had stolen the money in the first place and wanted it back.

Now what?

The desperate man catches up with them, and then . . .

The man's sweaty face broke into a smile as he slowed to push his way through the thin branches of a sapling.

"Sure," he said aloud. "Sure, that's it." His grin widened. The boys might be tough enough or brave enough to fight for the money—or for their lives. They might be willing to risk pain, injury, even death, in the struggle. But the one thing they would not risk—for sure—was the injury or death of the other one.

He needed only to menace one of the boys, and the other one would hand over the money.

"Simple, simple, simple," he told himself, still smiling.

The plan, once settled satisfactorily, seemed to give the man an added burst of energy, a renewed strength, and his jogging gait along the riverbank was almost a full-speed run when he saw the river widen and then open into Nina-Moose Lake.

He stopped and, breathing heavily, gazed out over the lake.

A red canoe was bobbing on the water in the middle of the lake.

THE WOODS
Todd and Mike

The breeze on Nina-Moose Lake was picking up, and Todd and Mike had to paddle hard to hold to their course. Tiny whitecaps rode the top of the rippling waves.

"It always seems like we're not getting anywhere paddling on a lake," Mike grunted from his seat in the bow of the canoe.

"The wind's not helping any," Todd said.

They dug the paddles deep into the water.

"Still nobody coming in," Todd said. "Funny."

"Yeah."

"Maybe the police know the hijacker is in this area, and they've sealed it off."

Neither of them spoke for a moment. Todd's guess at what was happening around them offered little comfort. The prospect of being alone in the woods with the hijacker in desperate pursuit of them—and no hope of encountering even other campers, much less police officers—set them to plowing the water deeper and faster with their paddles in dead silence.

The whacking noise of a helicopter broke the stillness

on the lake. Both boys quit paddling and turned their faces to the sky, but there was nothing but a soft blueness and the feathery wisps of white clouds moving in the breeze. Then the helicopter broke into sight over the tree-lined ridge to the right of them.

"There it is!" Mike shouted.

"Wave your paddle."

They both lifted their paddles and waggled the blades high in the air above their heads.

The helicopter headed toward them.

"There ought to be some kind of distress signal—you know, like SOS," Mike said. "Do you know?"

"Uh-huh."

They watched, continuing to wave their paddles, as the helicopter, now down low over the water, drew near. Its whirling blades churned the water.

"He's going to swamp us if he comes much closer," Mike said.

"I hope he knows what he's doing."

"He must see us."

"Sure."

The helicopter tilted slightly and veered its path in a semicircle around Todd and Mike. Then it came to a virtual halt in midair and hovered fifty yards off the port side of the canoe. A face was visible.

Todd suddenly shouted at Mike above the roar of the helicopter: "A pan! A pan! Get a pan out of the pack!"

Mike turned in the seat. "A what?"

"A *pan*—can you get a *pan* out of the pack? Quick!"

"A pan? What—?"

165

"We can signal with it," Todd shouted. "Just like a mirror—send SOS."

Mike understood. He nodded as he laid his paddle across the gunwales and twisted in his seat, reaching toward the pack behind him. He fumbled with the buckle of the huge Paul Bunyan pack and flipped the flap open, then struggled to move something inside the pack, and finally pulled out the utensil pack. He opened it and stuck his hand in.

"I've got it!" he shouted.

The helicopter tilted again and turned, and began moving away toward the far bank at the boys' left.

Mike had the glistening metal pan in his hand.

"Start flashing them," Todd shouted.

Mike held the pan in both hands. He tilted it back and forth with quick, jerky movements. Then he wiggled it from side to side.

Todd stared at the departing helicopter, as if his intent gaze alone could cause it to return, or at the least make the pilot give one final backward glance at the two boys in the red canoe. The signals themselves did not need to convey letters or words. The mere fact that they obviously were trying to signal the 'copter would be message enough. The pilot would know they were in distress. If only he would look back.

"He doesn't see it," Mike said.

"Keep going. He may look back."

The helicopter kept to its course, moving away from Todd and Mike, heading straight for the trees on the bank. Then it went up and over the trees and out of sight.

Todd, who had unconsciously kept his paddle blade in

the air, now brought it down and laid it in front of him across the gunwales. Mike, staring at the empty sky above the trees to his left, quit waggling the pan and held it in both hands in his lap. They sat, dead in the water, in silence for almost a full minute.

"Well," Todd said finally, "leave the pan out where you can get to it in case he comes back over."

"Uh-huh, sure."

They both picked up their paddles again and put the blades in the water.

Todd, turning his head to the right, sighted on a jutting rock at the bank. "If you want some more bad news," he said, "it looks like we lost yardage to the wind while we were waving at the chopper."

"Figures," Mike said. He bent forward and dug his paddle into the water.

"Wait a minute!"

"Huh?" Mike, startled by the tone of Todd's voice, twisted around in his seat and looked back.

"No, no, keep paddling," he said, lowering his head and taking a stroke with the paddle. "Act normal, but there's somebody moving around on the bank."

"Where?"

"Just paddle. He's to the right, a little behind us—but don't look. Just keep paddling."

Mike kept his face pointed straight ahead, paddling hard. Todd shifted his paddle from port to starboard, enabling him to turn his head with a natural movement of his body in the course of a stroke and scan the shore in the distance.

"See anything?" Mike asked without turning.

"No, not now. But I did a minute ago."

"A man, you mean? Or just some movement—maybe a bear or a deer?"

"If it was a bear," Todd said, taking a long reach forward and dipping the paddle blade deep into the water, "it was the first bear I ever saw wearing a khaki shirt."

THE WOODS
The Man

Ten yards in from the bank, the man sat with his back to a spruce tree and gazed through bushes into the bright glare of the morning sun above the eastern horizon, focusing on the red canoe.

The helicopter seemed to come out of nowhere and had almost caught him in the open. For a chilling moment, he thought for sure he had been spotted. But apparently not. Maybe the pilot's face was turned the other way. It didn't matter now. The chopper had moved out over the lake, hovered over the boys, and then disappeared in the opposite direction.

The boys had waved frantically at the helicopter. They obviously had tried to signal it, using a pan to reflect the sunlight. But the pilot either had not noticed or had not understood what he had seen and read from their actions. The wild waving of the paddles, and then the desperate attempt at mirror signaling, told the man beyond a doubt that his money was in the red canoe. He had figured that it must have been the boys who got his money. It was a logical conclusion, and he had acted on it. And now they, with their frantic efforts at signaling the helicopter, had told him that his logic had been correct. The man had thought he was on the right track. Now he knew it.

Had the boys seen him when he stumbled on the bank, almost tripping into the water? Probably so. The boy in the stern was facing this way. Then the one in the bow jerked around so fast he might have capsized the canoe. And then, quickly, they both bent to the business of paddling, with the one in the stern sneaking another glance. But even if they had spotted him, it didn't matter now. The race was on. And he still held control of the element of surprise—when and where to encounter the boys.

The man pulled the map from his pocket. He needed now only to move down the lake and along Moose River, parallel to the boys, until they came upon a portage. And then, while they were struggling along the path with heavy packs on their backs and the bulky canoe held over their heads . . .

He glanced down at the map. The river ran for a mile, maybe a mile and a half, before the first portage. The man grunted. He would have preferred a shorter distance—a shorter time—to the first portage. He was anxious to make his move, retrieve his money, resume his flight, and accomplish his escape. Every moment of delay, each extra step, was another moment of danger, another chance of exposure.

The map told the man something else, too: he was running out of space and time. The boys were moving dangerously close to the end of the streams and portages

leading out of the woods. They were moving dangerously close to Echo Trail, with its steady flow of campers
coming and going. If he held any hope of retrieving the
money and making his escape, he had to make his move
on the next portage trail. If not, he would have to settle
for escape—empty-handed. He could not afford to come
upon a group of campers.

Campers? The man frowned at the thought. There
were no canoeists coming in. He knew what that meant.
Police had sealed off the area. There were police waiting
on Echo Trail. For sure, he had to make his move quickly,
and then make his break—to the east or west, not to the
south toward Echo Trail.

The man got to his feet and replaced the map in his
shirt pocket. He took another glance at the red canoe
struggling against the wind on the lake, and began walking at a brisk pace through the woods.

Nothing to do now but keep the lakeshore and then the
riverbank to his left—and keep out of sight.

HEADQUARTERS
Agent Stoneham

For Ted Stoneham, leaning on the counter watching the radio operator conduct the normal business of the sheriff's office, the minutes dragged by.

Out there in the woods, Phil Schuyler was leading a group of state troopers and sheriff's deputies in tracking the trail of—who? Maybe a hijacker carrying three-quarters of a million dollars in two canvas bags. Or maybe an innocent camper doing some exploring, while the hijacker made good his escape in another direction. Either way, the trail was holding up. The latest radio report, relayed by a trooper staking out a takeout point, had the party advancing steadily and unmistakenly on the trail of —well, somebody.

The men in the pontoon plane on Lake Agnes had found the green canoe, fully equipped with gear, beneath the cover of two ground cloths held in place by rocks at the corners. Lars Nillsen noted again the oddity of a canoeist covering his canoe with ground cloths. There was only one explanation: to try to camouflage the canoe from searching eyes above. The men finding the canoe had reported another oddity, too: the food pack, containing several days' supply, was in the canoe, easy pickings for a foraging bear, instead of dangling safely from the end of a rope high in a tree. "Either the man planned to leave the canoe and gear and go on to another stash, or he was planning to head for a takeout point instead of going deeper into the woods and figured the food wasn't worth the trouble," Nillsen said. "Neither makes sense. And why all that food if he was planning to come out? It's our man's gear, you can bet on it."

Stoneham had replied with only a nod, silently reflecting that they seemed to be finding everything connected with the man except the money and the hijacker himself.

The helicopters crisscrossing the area reported in periodically, always with the same offering—nothing. They saw no trace of a lone man. And, with the officers blocking new campers from entering the area, they were deprived of even an occasional false alarm—a campsite, a canoeist—to report. Those heading in before the entries were sealed had paddled far into the interior by now, and, it being midweek, few if any of those in the interior were making their way toward a takeout point. The big exodus occurred on the weekends.

Stoneham turned away from the young deputy manning the radio and stared out the window at the traffic on the street. Almost every vehicle was either a pickup truck, a four-wheel-drive rough-duty car, or a recreational vehicle. Some of them pulled trailers. A surprising number carried canoes—silver, red, green, yellow, one even painted with wavy yellow and brown tiger stripes.

173

"You know," Stoneham said to Nillsen, "when all this is over, I'm going to come back up here one day and let you take me on a canoe camping trip."

"You should."

"Would you do it?"

"Sure."

Stoneham nodded slightly. "You've got a date," he said. "There must be something good about it—all of these people all over the place, hauling canoes and packs."

Nillsen grinned. "There *is* something good about it."

A voice crackled over the radio.

"It's Jacob," the operator siad.

Stoneham turned, and he and Nillsen leaned in to listen to the report from the helicopter.

"Nothing really," the voice said. "Just a couple of boys in a red canoe on Nina-Moose Lake. Paddling out, it looks like."

Stoneham glanced at Nillsen. The two boys in the red canoe were in the center of the ring. Nillsen had warned that there might be some paddlers and campers in the area, ignorant of the chase in progress, perhaps in danger. Until now, none had been spotted.

He looked down at the map under the cracked glass of the countertop. "Maybe we ought to send in a plane to lift them out of there," he said, speaking more to himself than to anyone else.

"If they were on the lake a few minutes ago they'll be off it now, moving along Moose River," Nillsen said. "There's no way to lift them out of there."

Stoneham frowned. Instincts born of a lifetime in police work told him to clear a danger area of all innocent parties. But probably Nillsen was right. The boys in the red canoe were on the river—or would be on it by the time a plane arrived—and out of reach of rescuers. "Yeah, okay," he said to Nillsen, and then turned to the radio operator. "Have them send a couple or three officers in to meet the boys coming out, will you?"

"Roger."

While the operator turned to his microphone, flipped a switch, and began relaying the message, Stoneham looked back at Nillsen. "I'm going out there. We're right on the edge of a break. I can feel it. Want to come?"

"Sure."

THE WOODS
Todd and Mike

"How much river have we got before the first portage?" Mike asked from his seat in the bow. "A lot, isn't it?" He had his head turned to catch the answer.

They had paddled the final strokes across the windblown lake and were gliding through the wide mouth of Moose River.

"Mile or so," Todd said.

"Well, then, less than an hour to the road—the takeout point—wouldn't you say?"

"Yeah, maybe an hour. We've got a couple of short portages and the final long one to the road."

"We could run it from the next portage. What do you think?"

"Uh-huh. If we have to. We'll see. But for now, we need to paddle."

They dug their paddles into the water. Ahead of them the river narrowed, bringing the wall of woods in close upon them.

Todd frowned at the sight. "Keep a sharp eye out up there," he said.

"I am."

The canoe sliced through the water easily and silently. The woods on both sides were still and quiet.

"Here's the beaver dam coming up," Mike said.

Todd looked up. Beyond Mike's shoulder he saw the tangle of sticks stretching from bank to bank, blocking the stream. He remembered the dam and the squishy mud Mike brought up when he thrust his paddle to the bottom of the shallow water. That was on the other side of the dam, but the streambed was surely the same on this side. "Let's take it on the left, at the bank, like we did yesterday," Todd said.

"Right."

The bow of the canoe bumped the dam. Shoving against the dam with his paddle, Mike nosed the canoe toward the bank. Todd, paddling, brought the stern into line. They stepped out onto the bank, and, with Mike pulling and Todd shoving, they scraped the canoe over the dam and settled it in the water on the other side. Todd stepped around and steadied the canoe while Mike boarded.

The noise was not loud, but in the quiet of the woods it seemed like the crack of a rifle shot. Todd looked up quickly and peered into the woods in the direction of the sound. Through the trees and bushes he saw a quick flash of khaki—visible and then gone.

Mike seated himself in the bow, turned, and looked toward the sound. "What was that?" His voice was barely above a hiss.

"Him," Todd whispered. "I saw him."

As if waiting for another snapping sound from the woods, or perhaps a flash of khaki in the wall of green, the boys remained motionless—Todd bending over the gunwales, ready to step into the canoe, and Mike seated in the bow, his body turned toward the sound.

"Where do you think he is?" Mike's voice was a whisper.

"I don't know."

"Let's go get him," Mike said. "We can take him."

Todd took his eyes off the woods and looked at Mike. Maybe Mike was right. The two of them could chase the man down, subdue him, hold him at knifepoint, and tie him up. The threat would be ended.

"No," Todd said finally. "The longer he plays cat and mouse with us, the closer we are to getting out of here, or running into somebody. Anyway, this is better than running into a gun or a knife."

Mike glanced at Todd briefly, then said, "Yeah, okay."

"So let's get going."

Todd shoved off the canoe and stepped in, and the boys, with deep paddle strokes, sent the canoe shooting forward in the stream.

The woods on both sides were silent and still as they bent to their work, digging the paddles deep into the water, heading toward the short portage that awaited them a mile away.

Once they heard a helicopter—at first barely audible, and then louder, and then only faintly, and finally nothing, just silence again. They scanned the sky but never saw it.

"Do you think he's out in front of us now?" Mike asked over his shoulder.

"Maybe."

"We should've gone after him. Now he's getting to pick his spot."

Todd frowned. "Maybe so," he said.

They reached the start of the portage path and leaped out of the canoe, dragged it onto the rocky bank, and leaned in to pull out the packs.

"We're never going to make it past this portage without meeting him," Mike said, looking at the still woods across the stream, knowing they hid the man. "This is where he's got to make his move. We're getting too close to getting out. He can't wait any longer."

Todd nodded. "I think you're right."

"What are we going to do?"

"We could make a run for it from here."

"Let's go. It's a better chance than getting caught with a ton of gear strapped on our backs and a canoe over our heads."

"But the money," Todd said. "We can't just leave it."

"We never should have rolled it up in the sleeping bags. If it was in the canvas bags, we could just—"

"Wait a minute," Todd said. He opened one of the packs, fumbled his hand around inside for a moment, then opened the other pack. Glancing up to make sure the man was not in sight, perhaps even approaching them, he extracted the two canvas bags that had held the money. He put them on the ground, hidden by the canoe from the woods across the stream.

"What are you doing?"

"Let's fill them with rocks or dirt or something—make them look full . . . heavy." He glanced across the stream at the woods again, and then bent over the bags, stuffing them with fist-sized rocks. "C'mon, hurry, and keep the bags down behind the canoe."

"I don't get it."

"If he sees us running away with these bags, he's not going to worry about what we've left behind in the canoe —like the sleeping bags, you know."

"But what if he's watching us now?"

Todd sighed. "Then the trick won't work. C'mon, hurry." He closed the flap and zipped it shut. "Ready?"

Mike zipped the other flap shut. "Yeah."

Todd hesitated.

"What's wrong?"

"Once we leave the canoe behind, the jig is up. He will know that we've spotted him."

"He probably knows we've spotted him anyway."

"But for sure he won't play cat and mouse with us any longer. He'll come after us."

"I think I'd be able to run pretty fast."

"But, like I said, the longer we can stall him into playing the cat and mouse game with us, the closer we'll get to the takeout point, and the shorter the run we'll have to make." Todd paused. "I can't help thinking that he might be armed. After all, you know, he hijacked an airliner."

"Yeah, but—"

"Look, let's load up, just like everything was normal,

and walk the portage. If we reach the end without meeting him, we'll be back in the water, and that much farther ahead."

"But what if we do meet him?"

Todd shrugged. "We can always throw the canoe at him."

"Okay," Mike said finally.

"And then we can drop our packs and run—with the money bags. He won't stop to see what we've left behind."

"Okay, okay. I guess so."

They grabbed the packs out of the canoe and hoisted them onto their backs, pulling the straps tight. Next they draped the canvas money bags filled with rocks over their shoulders. Tying the paddles to the struts, they rolled the canoe up their bodies and into position above their heads.

"Set?"

"Set."

THE WOODS
The Man

He heard the sound of the helicopter, but the noise began to fade almost immediately and he did not bother to dive for cover. He continued to plunge ahead.

He was far back from the river, probably more than fifty yards, near the top of a rise in the ground. He had moved back up the slope after a sudden bend in the river had left him thrashing through the woods almost at the riverbank. As luck would have it, the boys were there, dragging their canoe over a beaver dam. He had seen them look up in alarm at the loud crack of a breaking stick. Probably they had seen him as clearly as he had seen them. It didn't really matter, of course, but if he was going to intercept them on the next portage, it was better he remain unseen until the last moment.

He stepped up his pace as best he could in the untracked tangle of woods. He needed to beat the boys to the portage path so that he could have a look around and pick his spot. On the river, the boys were sure to make better time than he was, shoving his way through bushes and circling clumps of trees. The boys no longer had the stiff breeze of Nina-Moose Lake to slow them down, and he couldn't count on many obstacles, such as the beaver dam, to hinder their progress. He had to keep going— faster, faster, faster.

His breath was coming in great gulps and the perspiration was streaming down his face when he suddenly halted, knowing somehow that he had reached the area of the portage path.

He stood still a moment, his chest heaving with the effort of breathing, and then turned to his left, down the hill, toward the slow waters of Moose River.

He reached back with his right hand and touched the hunting knife in the scabbard on his hip.

THE WOODS
Agent Stoneham

The brown car with the white lettering "Sheriff" on the door and the red lights on top, on loan to Ted Stoneham for the duration, turned off the dirt road and came to a halt in the dusty parking area.

A half-dozen pickup trucks and cars were parked in a row along one side of the lot, awaiting the return of their owners from the interior of the BWCA.

On the other side of the parking area two state police cars stood, their driver's-side doors open, giving off the unmistakable sounds of police radios. Four troopers and five other men were standing between the two cars. Across the road a couple of teenagers sat amid a collection of packs, next to a car with the canoe still tied tightly in place on the roof. Doubtless they were frustrated victims of the police blockade, waiting for the signal that they could enter and, in the meantime, just watching to see what might happen.

Stoneham got out of the brown car on the passenger side. Nillsen emerged from the driver's side. They walked to the group of men between the two state police cars.

Stoneham took his badge wallet out of his hip pocket and opened it to the officers. "Stoneham, FBI," he said.

"Yes, sir," one of the officers said.

One of the civilians—either a deputy sheriff or a ranger, Stoneham figured—looked at Nillsen and said, "Hi, Lars."

Nillsen nodded.

"Anything?" Stoneham asked. "Anything at all?"

One of the troopers shook his head.

"Nothing on the two boys in the red canoe who are on their way out?"

"Trooper Johnson and a couple of deputies have gone in to meet them. Haven't heard anything yet."

"Those boys may have seen something," Stoneham said.

"Yeah."

A helicopter swept out of the woods, circled over the parking area, and roared back into the woods, disappearing behind the trees. Silence returned to the woods.

Stoneham and Nillsen walked to the head of the path leading into the woods—the long portage to the first navigable stretch of Moose River—and stared at the emptiness along the corridor between the trees.

"Now we wait," Stoneham said.

THE WOODS
Todd and Mike

Ten paces down the path they heard the unmistakable sound of dead branches snapping under the weight of a man's foot. The sound came from ahead of them and to the right, across the rock-filled stream running parallel to the portage path. The man was coming toward them through the woods.

Todd lifted the canoe to obtain a line of sight and peered beyond Mike's right shoulder. He saw the man come out of the woods and step into the river.

At that instant Mike uttered a low, "Uh-oh."

Todd whispered, "I see him."

The man, watching them, picked his way through the rocks in the knee-deep water and stepped up to the edge of the path, ahead of Mike and to his right.

Todd and Mike kept walking, drawing close to him.

"Oh, hi, there," Mike sang out. He did a good job of making the greeting sound cheerful, casual, unworried.

The man held a hunting knife in his right hand.

Mike, at the front, was less than six feet from him. He slowed to a halt and Todd, at the rear, stopped with him.

For a moment—nothing. All three of them—the man, Mike, Todd—stood motionless in the quiet stillness of the woods.

The man's eyes were fixed on the canvas bag slung over Mike's shoulder. Then he looked at the bag on Todd's shoulder.

He brought the knife up to waist high, extended it, and waggled the blade slightly, shifting his gaze from Todd to Mike and back to Todd again, finally settling on Mike, the one nearest him.

Todd watched the glistening knife blade move in the sunlight. He noticed a tensing of the muscles in Mike's arms, back, legs.

"You give me the money," the man said slowly, spacing the words, "and there won't be any trouble."

Todd felt Mike's short forward tug on the canoe. Mike wanted to throw it.

"Put down the canoe and give me the money, and there won't be any trouble," the man repeated.

Todd shouted, "One-two-*three*"—in rapid-fire order.

The man tensed, then started to crouch, bracing himself, seeming to know what was coming.

At the shout of "three" they pitched the canoe.

The man was a second too late in bracing himself. The canoe went into him broadside and chest high. He threw up an arm—the one with the knife held in the hand—to protect himself. The canoe crashed into him with the sharp sound—*thump!*—of metal hitting bone. The knife flew as if thrown into the air, and sailed into the river. The weight of the canoe sent the man stumbling backward, and he fell to the ground beneath it, one foot in the river. He scrambled furiously to throw off the canoe and regain his feet. The foot in the water skidded on the slippery bottom and he fell back.

Todd and Mike shucked their Paul Bunyan packs and dashed around him. They headed down the portage path toward a bend that would put them out of sight, if only for a second or two.

Todd, for good measure, shouted ahead to Mike as loud as he could, "*Don't drop the money.*"

Mike looked back as he ran and laughed.

The path bent to the right, putting them out of the man's sight, and then back to the left—and ended. The short portage was at an end. The river was navigable again. The boys stopped at the water's edge. They looked at the riverbank ahead. It was steep and forested on both sides—certainly no place for running. They looked at the water, two to three feet deep. It would be slow going.

"Into the water," Todd said.

"No, no. Wait a minute."

"What?"

"Let's take him. We can do it. His knife's gone. No gun."

Todd grinned at his friend. "You're just dying for a little physical contact, aren't you?"

"Okay then?"

"Okay."

They dropped the canvas bags on the ground and moved back down the path, toward the first of the two bends between them and the place where they had left the man scrambling beneath the canoe.

In the quiet of the woods they heard the man, out of sight, running toward them—pounding footbeats on the hard-packed portage trail.

"Here he comes," Mike said. "Let's go."

"Wait a minute," Todd said, stopping. "Is that somebody shouting?"

"Yo!" came a shout from their right and behind them. "Who's there?"

The man came charging around the bend into view. At the sound of the call from the woods, he skidded to a halt. His eyes darted from Todd to Mike, and then beyond, toward the woods where an unseen man had called out.

Ten yards away from Todd and Mike, the man crouched like a cornered animal.

"Who's that?" Todd shouted over his shoulder.

"Police officers. Don't move."

The man, his voice low and husky, said, "Give me the money."

"Where are you?" came the shout from the woods.

"Here! Here! *Here!*" Todd shouted.

The man straighted, paused a moment, and ran back the way he had come, out of sight around the bend.

Todd and Mike suddenly were surrounded by three men—a trooper in uniform and two men in khaki wearing deputy sheriff badges.

"That way—that way—he was just here—he went that way, down the path," Todd shouted.

"Who?"

"The hijacker."

The two deputies took off at a dead run, pistols in their hands.

Todd turned to the trooper. "We've got the money," he said.

The trooper looked at Todd without changing expression. "You have?"

HEADQUARTERS
Todd and Mike

Todd and Mike placed their tightly rolled sleeping bags on the end of the long table in the headquarters room at the rear of Barney's Restaurant.

Ted Stoneham and Lars Nillsen were on either side of them. All along the table, men dressed in various types of law enforcement uniforms stood and watched. And behind them on one side of the table, Barney and one of his waitresses peered at the scene past the shoulders of the men.

The time was almost noon, almost an hour after Todd and Mike had met the officers on the portage path. The hijacker, captured after a quick chase through the woods, was locked in a cell at the rear of the sheriff's office across the street. Todd and Mike, standing with Ted Stoneham in the parking area, had watched the officers bring him out of the woods, handcuffed, and load him into a patrol car for the fast drive into town.

Their trip into Ely, like the man's, was accompanied by wailing sirens and flashing lights.

At Barney's Restaurant, officers had held back the

newspaper reporters, television cameramen, and gawking townspeople, while hustling Todd and Mike, each clutching a sleeping bag, inside.

The room was quiet as Todd loosened the final knot and pulled the end of the rope through. He gave the rolled-up bag a slight shove and it unrolled on the table, displaying row after row of decks of currency. Mike finished untying his bag at the same time and unrolled it, too. Again, row after row after row of taped packets of currency were revealed.

One of the men at the other end of the table gave a low whistle. Everyone stared at the money—three-quarters of a million dollars.

"Well, there it is," Todd said with a shrug.

"Yes," Stoneham said. He looked from the money to Todd and Mike. "Part of it is yours, you know."

"What do you mean?" Todd asked.

"The insurance company was offering a reward of twenty-five thousand dollars for information leading to the arrest of the hijacker, or for the return of the money. You boys qualify for the reward."

"Really?" Todd said.

"Oh, wow," Mike said.

Todd glanced at Mike. He was thinking about the night before, when they had discussed keeping the money for themselves. They both had been tempted, even though it had been Mike who'd put the suggestion into words. Now, looking at his friend, Todd knew the same memories were flashing through Mike's mind. Neither of them spoke.

"What will you do with all that money—twelve thousand five-hundred dollars apiece?" Stoneham asked.

The two boys spoke the word together: "College."

"Well, you earned it. You were honest in bringing the money in. You were brave in taking chances with a man you knew to be a desperate hijacker. And you showed a lot of presence of mind—a lot of cleverness—in rolling up the money in the sleeping bags."

"Well, I—" Todd stammered.

"It was Todd's idea to hide the money in the sleeping bags," Mike said.

"Well, it was a good one," Stoneham said. "What do you two want to do now?"

"Now?" Todd glanced at Mike. "I guess we'd better call our folks."

Stoneham smiled. "I think that's a good idea. They're going to be seeing you on television and reading about you in the papers when those reporters outside get through with you."

"Wow," Mike said. "We'll be on television."

"And then," Todd said, glancing back at Mike, "I think what we'd like to do is go back into the woods and finish our trip."

Mike nodded his agreement. "That's what we came up here for in the first place—a nice, quiet canoe camping trip in the nice, quiet BWCA."

The remark brought a round of soft laughter from the men standing around the table.

Stoneham, smiling, said, "We'll try this time to keep the woods free of hijackers."

The room was silent a moment.

Then Todd said, "But first, I was wondering . . ."

"Yes?"

"Could we get something to eat? We missed breakfast, and—"

"Yeah," Mike interrupted. "A couple of hamburgers would go pretty good."

"Comin' up," Barney said, "and it's on the house—and with fries, too. Okay?"

Todd grinned. "Yeah, great."

ABOUT THE AUTHOR

Thomas J. Dygard was born in Little Rock, Arkansas, and received a B.A. degree from the University of Arkansas, Fayetteville. He began his career as a sportswriter for the *Arkansas Gazette* in Little Rock and joined the Associated Press in 1954. Since then he has worked in A.P. offices in Little Rock, Detroit, Birmingham, New Orleans, and Indianapolis. At present, he is Bureau Chief in Chicago.

Mr. Dygard is married, has two children, and now lives in Arlington Heights, Illinois.